"I MADE YOU A PROMISE, FARGO . . ."

Her hands came up to slide around his neck. "You came for me. You are a man of your word, Fargo, and I keep my promises."

Fargo thought of the others waiting. They could wait a little longer, he murmured silently. He lifted her up with a sweep of his arms, put her down on the cool grass. She made a motion with one hand, pulling at strings, and the peasant blouse came undone and she flung it over her head. Fargo let his eyes appreciate the full beauty of her for a moment. Smiling as he reached for her, Fargo had to agree that some promises just had to be fulfilled . . .

Wild Westerns From SIGNET

- [ ] **RUFF JUSTICE #1: SUDDEN THUNDER by Warren T. Longtree.** (#AE1029—$2.50)
- [ ] **RUFF JUSTICE #2: NIGHT OF THE APACHE by Warren T. Longtree.** (#AE1028—$2.50)
- [ ] **THE TRAILSMAN #1: SEVEN WAGONS WEST by Jon Sharpe.** (#AE1052—$2.25)
- [ ] **THE TRAILSMAN #2: THE HANGING TRAIL by Jon Sharpe.** (#AE1053—$2.25)
- [ ] **THE TRAILSMAN #3: MOUNTAIN MAN KILL by Jon Sharpe.** (#AE1130—$2.25)
- [ ] **THE TRAILSMAN #4: THE SUNDOWN SEARCHERS by Jon Sharpe.** (#AE1158—$2.25)
- [ ] **THE TRAILSMAN #5: THE RIVER RAIDERS by Jon Sharpe.** (#AE1199—$2.25)
- [ ] **THE TRAILSMAN #6: DAKOTA WILD by Jon Sharpe.** (#E9777—$2.25)
- [ ] **THE TRAILSMAN #7: WOLF COUNTRY by Jon Sharpe.** (#E9905—$2.25)
- [ ] **THE TRAILSMAN #8: SIX-GUN DRIVE by Jon Sharpe.** (#AE1024—$2.25)

THE TRAILSMAN 9

DEAD MAN'S SADDLE

by
Jon Sharpe

Ⓢ
A SIGNET BOOK
NEW AMERICAN LIBRARY
TIMES MIRROR

NAL BOOKS ARE AVAILABLE AT QUANTITY DISCOUNTS WHEN USED TO PROMOTE PRODUCTS OR SERVICES. FOR INFORMATION PLEASE WRITE TO PREMIUM MARKETING DIVISION, THE NEW AMERICAN LIBRARY, INC., 1633 BROADWAY, NEW YORK, NEW YORK 10019.

The first chapter of this book appeared in
SIX-GUN DRIVE, the eighth volume in this series.

SIGNET TRADEMARK REG. U.S. PAT. OFF. AND FOREIGN COUNTRIES
REGISTERED TRADEMARK—MARCA REGISTRADA
HECHO EN CHICAGO, U.S.A.

SIGNET, SIGNET CLASSICS, MENTOR, PLUME, MERIDIAN AND NAL BOOKS are published by The New American Library, Inc., 1633 Broadway, New York, New York 10019

First Printing, January, 1982

1 2 3 4 5 6 7 8 9

PRINTED IN THE UNITED STATES OF AMERICA

The Trailsman

Beginnings . . . they bend the tree and they mark the man. Skye Fargo was born when he was eighteen. Terror was his midwife, vengeance his first cry. Killing spawned Skye Fargo, ruthless, cold-blooded murder. Out of the acrid smoke of gunpowder still hanging in the air, he rose, cried out a promise never forgotten.

The Trailsman, they began to call him all across the West, searcher, scout, hunter, the man who could see where others only looked, his skills for hire but not his soul, the man who lived each day to the fullest, yet trailed each tomorrow. Skye Fargo, the Trailsman, the seeker who could take the wildness of a land and the wanting of a woman and make them his own.

The town of Condor,
where the Texas Territory and
Mexico nudged each other.

1

Fargo opened the door to the hotel room and halted in surprise. They'd told him he had a visitor waiting, but he'd expected the army sergeant making another pitch. He let his eyebrows lift as he took in the girl, deep strawberry-blond hair pulled back a little severely, tall, long legs enclosed in riding britches, a buckskin vest over a tan blouse that couldn't completely hold down the soft curve of full breasts. He scanned her face—deeply tanned, a nice nose, full lips, soft blue eyes, a pretty face able to look very firm and businesslike, as it did now.

"Sorry to surprise you like this," she said, her voice low, and she allowed a little smile to soften her face. "I've come to try to persuade you," she said.

"The army send you?" He frowned incredulously.

"No, I'm here on my own account. I'm Fern Blake," she said.

His eyes took in her figure again, returned to her face. Very nice, he decided. "How do you figure to persuade me?" he asked. "With clothes on or clothes off?"

He saw her lips draw in for a moment. "With clothes on," she said coolly.

"That's going to make it a lot harder." He smiled amiably.

1

"A thousand dollars," she said, "That ought to take care of persuading."

Fargo let his eyes study her.

"What do you say?" she asked.

"I say I'm getting curious as all hell," he answered. "First this apple-cheeked young sergeant comes up and tells me the army wants me to do a job for them, double the usual civilian scout's pay. I tell him I'm not interested, and he says it's my patriotic duty and he's authorized to make it triple the usual pay. Now you're here offering a hell of a lot more . . . only you're not the army; you're here on your own."

"It must be somewhat unsettling." She smiled. She was trying to be coolly pleasant, he saw, but something bubbled deep inside her. He caught the way her fingers moved nervously on the edge of the small leather purse she had over one shoulder.

"I don't unsettle easy, but why don't you tell me what the hell this is all about, honey," he said.

"Fern Blake," she corrected.

"All right, Fern. That's a nice name. Now talk," he said.

She looked uncomfortable for a moment. "You were told it was a scouting assignment. That's all I can say until you agree to take the job," she said.

"Then you can go persuade somebody else, Fern, honey," he said affably.

"There is no one like you. You are the best, I'm told," she said. He shrugged, made no comment. "I've offered a lot of money," she said.

"You have," he agreed. "But then, money never did persuade me much about anything."

She shot him a distinctly annoyed frown. "Are you saying that if I persuaded you with my clothes off you'd agree?" she asked.

2

"No, but I'd enjoy it more," he said. "Try me." He smiled. "You never know."

"I have the impression you're more interested in that than the job," she said disapprovingly.

"You get the cigar, honey." He smiled.

"Fern," she snapped.

"Fern," he said agreeably.

He saw her shrug in dismay, her hand move under the buckskin vest. It came out holding a small pistol, a rim-fire European model, but deadly enough at this close range. "I'm afraid I'll have to use this kind of persuasion, then," she said.

He eyed the gun again. "You're full of surprises, aren't you?" he said.

"Take your gun from the holster," she ordered. "Use two fingers only." She backed a few paces, kept the little pistol leveled at him. "The gun, please," Fern Blake said sharply.

"You won't use that popgun, honey," Fargo said calmly.

"I certainly will," she retorted indignantly.

He shook his head. "I can't do you much good dead, now, can I?" he said affably, saw her mouth fall open for a second. It was a reply she hadn't thought about. She blinked, the gun still on him, and he heard the sound of footsteps approaching in the hallway, two pairs of boots. His hand went to the holster. "They come in this room they're dead men," he said.

He saw Fern Blake hesitate, and then her voice called out sharply. "No, stay there. Don't come in," she said.

"You in trouble?" Fargo heard the voice call out.

"No," the girl said. "I'm all right. Stay outside." Fargo heard the quiver in her voice, uncertainty and dismay in it. The men outside caught it, also. His eyes were on the door as it crashed open, the two men rushing in after it, guns in hand. Fargo had the big Colt in his hand before

3

the door had half-opened. He fired, twice, the two shots so fast they seemed one. The two men hit each other as they fell backward, collapsing into the hallway with twin stains of red spreading from their chests.

Fargo turned to Fern Blake, the Colt in his hand. She was staring out at the two figures lying half atop each other in the hallway, her face white, drawn, "I told them to let me handle it," she gasped out. "I told them."

"They should have listened to you," Fargo said casually. "Now give me that popgun." She brought her eyes to him and he saw refusal there. "I can make it three," he said.

"You wouldn't," she gasped out, watched his eyes, and swallowed hard, reached her hand out to give him the gun. He flipped it on its side, emptied the two shells, and tossed it back to her. More footsteps pounded outside and others appeared in the hallway. He saw a figure push its way through, a beefy man wearing a sheriff's badge.

"They tried to rob the lady and me," Fargo said, glanced at Fern Blake.

She blinked, shook her head. "Yes, yes, that's right," she said.

The sheriff looked down at the two men. "Anybody know them?" he asked. No one answered. "Never saw them before, either," the man grumbled. "All right, get 'em out of here."

Fargo grunted as he shut the door. Condor was a town that was like this land, a place where life and death were only passing moments. There was law, but not much of it. Mostly there was the fight to find a place to survive in a land that was still torn between two countries, a place of divided loyalties and no loyalties at all. He'd led a party of land speculators down here and he had no desire to stay. He turned to Fern Blake.

"Now you can start persuading me with your clothes off," he said.

Her eyes grew wide, fear leaping in their soft blue centers. "No, you wouldn't," she said.

"Either that or you start telling me what the hell this is all about," he barked.

She drew a deep breath and the tan vest moved an inch out farther. "All right," she almost whispered. "But not here, not now. Tonight. I want somebody else there to meet you," she said. "I'm staying at little place just south of Condor. Ride along Mesa Road and you can't miss it."

"If you're trying to set me up again, you're going to be the prettiest corpse this side of the border," Fargo said harshly. Her eyes were wide, but he saw no duplicity in them. Her hand reached out, touched his for a moment, drew back at once.

"No tricks, I promise," she said. "I'm sorry about this, all of it. It just went all wrong, even my part. It was a bad idea, all of it," she said.

"I'd agree with that," he said.

"Nine o'clock," she said, and he nodded. She moved to the door, paused, looked back at him. She was really damn good-looking, he decided, and wondered what in hell she was into. "I'm sorry, really I am," she offered.

"We'll see," was all he allowed her. He watched her strawberry-blond head disappear out the door, heard her footsteps hurrying down the hall. He lay down on the bed and waited for the night. Maybe she'd change her mind about how to persuade him.

2

Mesa Road followed the thin line of the moon and he rode slowly, unhurriedly. He'd waited till dark had wrapped itself around the town and the night sounds shuffled through Condor, mostly from the dance hall. Like most border towns, Condor had a distinctive character of its own, borrowing from both sides of the border, which existed only on a dusty map in a dusty government file someplace. The dance hall followed along with the rest of the town, the girls as much Mexican and part-Indian as American. It gave the place its own flavor, not that anyone here much cared, but one becomes an expert on dance halls when you ride trail long enough, Fargo reflected. A dubious achievement, he grunted wryly, turned the pinto along a curve in the road.

Fargo patted the pinto alongside the neck and the horse neighed softly in answer. Even in the dim light of the new moon, the pinto gleamed, an Ovaro with forequarters and hindquarters of jet black and a midsection of sparkling white. None who saw it forgot it, just as they didn't forget the rider with the black hair, the intense, handsome face with the lake-blue eyes, the body that sat the horse as if they were part of each other. Fargo's eyes swept the darkness of the road ahead, caught the faint glimmer of yellow light, moved toward it until the small house came into view, a few hundred feet from the road, tucked away in a rock-lined hollow. The window was shuttered, but a scattering of yellow escaped around the edges and Fargo noiselessly slid from the saddle. He left the pinto waiting as he moved forward in a half-crouch, the lake-blue eyes narrowed as they swept the rocks, peering into every dark place, watching for a movement, a sign, a shadowed shape. Finally, satisfied no one waited in the shadows, he returned, led the pinto after him as he moved to the little house, hardly more than a cabin.

He knocked on the door and had but a second to wait as it was opened and Fern stood there, her strawberry hair glinting in the light behind her. She wore a white blouse that swelled fully, tightening around the full undersides of her breasts. Her face, softened in the lamplight, was still as pretty as he remembered.

"I was beginning to wonder if you'd decided not to come," she said.

"I said I'd be here," he answered flatly.

She stepped back to let him enter and closed the door after him. The room was sparely furnished with only a puncheon table and two pine chairs. A man rose from one of them, of medium height, clothed in a well-tailored, brown frock coat with matching cravat. Fargo noted the brown-felt hat on the table. The man had gray-flecked hair over an even-featured face distinguished only by an air of weary patience in it. He rose to his feet.

"I'm Robert Boswell," he said, and Fargo acknowledged him with a short nod. The man tried a smile. Like his face, it held nothing but a kind of mechanicalness. "I'm afraid I must share in the blame for this afternoon's unpleasantness," he said. "Fern wanted to meet with you alone. I insisted those two men go along. A piece of mistaken protectiveness, I'm afraid."

"Yep," Fargo agreed curtly.

"But going to see you was my idea," Fern cut in.

"I don't much care," Fargo said. "The afternoon's done with."

He saw the girl blink and nod at the brusque impatience in his words. She had nice lips, he noted again, full, well-shaped, a mouth made for a lot more than talking. "Yes, of course," she said. "You've come to hear what this is all about. This afternoon, you asked if the army had sent me."

"And you said you were on your own," Fargo answered.

"Yes, but we both more or less want the same thing," Fern Blake told him.

"You and the army?" Fargo queried, lifting one thick black eyebrow.

"Yes, we want you to find a saddle for us," she said.

Fargo felt the frown slide over his face as he stared at her. "You bring me out here to make jokes?" he growled.

She shook her head and the strawberry-blond hair sent out little glints of coppery light. "No joke. It's a very special saddle, special in a lot of ways."

"Tell me some of them," Fargo said, unable to keep sarcasm from his voice.

Boswell cut in to answer. "Miss Blake's father made it. He's a master saddlemaker, an artist in leather. He learned the trade with the great saddlemakers who came from Mexico and whose families brought the art with them from Spain."

"Mr. Boswell bought the saddle from my father," Fern cut in.

"For a considerable amount of money," Boswell added.

"It was in my father's shop for some last-minute work when it was stolen," Fern went on. "Naturally, Mr.

Boswell wants the saddle or his money back, but my father had spent the money. He sent it to a sister in Massachusetts for an operation." Fern paused, glanced at Boswell, drew a deep breath. "So, the only thing was to get the saddle back. I set out to do that and Mr. Boswell decided to go along with me."

"You see, we know who stole it," Boswell said. "A man named Antonez. He was a dealer in all sorts of stolen goods, a very clever man. He stole the saddle because he knew what kind of a price it'd fetch from the right buyer. But now it grows more complicated. Antonez was killed and the saddle taken from him. There were eyewitnesses. It was a man named Vilas and two of his cronies. It's this Vilas we want. He has the saddle now."

"Interesting," Fargo commented blandly. "But where does the army fit in?"

"I'd rather they told you that," Boswell said. "Lieutenant Vander is in charge of the detail. I can tell you that he's not experienced in this area and he was authorized to hire help in tracking Vilas. That's why he sent his sergeant to see you."

Fargo nodded, let his lips purse. "Fern wants the saddle, you want the saddle, the army wants it. Anybody else?"

"Matter of fact, there is," Boswell said, and Fargo did not look surprised. "There are two agents from the First Southern Bank."

"What's their story?" Fargo questioned.

"Again, I'd rather leave them tell you," Boswell said.

Fern's voice cut in. "The important thing is that we get the saddle back. Everyone's agreed to contribute to paying for your fee in tracking Vilas for us," she said. "We have a few leads for you. We know he passed through Condor."

Fargo let his eyes go from Fern to Boswell. The man's

9

face remained one of weary patience. He'd make a good poker player, Fargo commented silently, only his eyes betraying him. They were sharp and full of anxiety. Fargo returned his glance to the girl, let it linger on the strawberry-blond hair, travel along the graceful line of her neck, down to the way her breasts swelled up at the top of the blouse. She met his glance. "We can raise the offer some," she slid out.

"It's not the money," Fargo said. "I feel like relaxing, not chasing all over the borderland." He let a rueful smile edge his lips. "But it sure as hell is a different kind of job. Sort of challenging," he remarked almost idly.

He saw her face break into hope. "Then you'll take it on?" she asked.

"I'll think about it," he answered, and watched her face flood with instant disappointment.

"I'm afraid time is most important," Boswell said.

"I'll tell you by noon tomorrow. I'll come by then," Fargo said.

"Mind if I have the others here? They'll want to know," Boswell asked.

"No matter to me." Fargo shrugged. He turned, started for the door, and found Fern going outside with him. "You coming out to persuade me some more?" he asked mildly.

"Not the way you mean," she said at once.

"Too bad. I feel like a warm woman and a cold bottle," he said.

"You'll be able to buy an awful lot of that for a thousand dollars," Fern said, a touch of disapproval creeping into her tone.

"What makes you think I *buy* that?" he asked.

Her eyes studied him. "I was wrong, then. I suppose you don't. Some women fancy your kind of animal attraction."

"You don't." He grinned.

"It's crude," she snapped.

"You mean it's honest. No games, no masks," he countered.

"Are you implying I'm being dishonest because I don't choose to persuade you that way?" she bristled.

"I wouldn't say a thing like that, not yet." Fargo smiled amiably.

"Not yet?" she said, a touch suspiciously.

"Meaning I haven't been around you long enough to know. Finding out about a woman is like walking through an apple orchard," he said, and saw the tiny frown touch her forehead. "Most of them look pretty good on the outside, but some are sweet and some are sour and some are all bitter and shriveled up inside. You have to find out which is which."

"And how do you do that?"

"You have to get into them, take a bite." He grinned back.

Her eyes narrowed again for a moment. "There are some apples you can't reach," she said.

"Never found one yet," Fargo returned mildly. He halted at the pinto and Fern Blake's glance went to the horse.

"A magnificent animal," she remarked.

"Maybe he needs a fancy saddle," Fargo said.

"I'm sure that could be included in your fee. My father has some on hand," the girl said quickly.

"Tell me, why didn't your pa come with you instead of Boswell?" Fargo questioned, keeping his tone casual.

"My father walks with a cane and he doesn't ride anymore, thanks to a mean, Mexican-bred buckskin," she answered as Fargo swung onto the pinto. Her blue eyes grew soft. "Please help us," she said. "Find your warm woman and cold bottle tonight and go with us tomorrow."

Fargo let a short, almost harsh laugh escape him. "I

was figuring on at least a week of relaxing, not one night," he said. He turned the pinto, looked back at her for another moment. "You're a pretty little piece, but you don't know much about some things, I'll wager," he remarked.

He saw her lips tighten, the soft blue eyes grow harder. "Noon, tomorrow," she said stiffly.

He laughed again and rode away, aware her eyes followed until he was out of sight in the dark. A small smile took hold of the corners of his mouth as he rode under the thin moon and there was an edge of ice in it. The offer intrigued him but not because it was a challenge as he'd let on to Fern and Boswell. They'd lied to him and he was becoming certain the army would hand him a lie, too, and the two men from the First Southern Bank. But that saddle was valuable, a hell of a lot more valuable than Fern and Boswell had let on. All of which meant it was worth a damnsight more than they were offering him to find it for them. Fargo uttered a short laugh in the night. He'd take their job, just long enough for him to get his hands on the saddle for himself. Then he'd do some real bargaining. They'd pay for trying to sell him a bill of goods, one or the other or all of them.

His eyes grew narrow in thought as he reached the outskirts of Condor. They'd combined forces to hire him. Had they combined lies, too? Or were they feeding each other tall tales, as well? He laughed quietly. It'd be interesting finding out. Only one thing was for sure: that saddle was very damn important to all of them. He passed the dance hall, slowed, then pulled the pinto to a halt. He dismounted and went into the oasis of light and tinkly noise in the night. A big woman saw him enter, started toward him at once, her manner if not her size marking her position in the dance hall.

"Hello, big feller," she began in a voice that still held the echo of a purr in it. But only an echo, most of it muted brass. "Looking for a good time?" She smiled out of lips too thickly painted.

"I want to talk to one of your girls," Fargo said.

She lifted one heavily penciled eyebrow. "Talk? You don't look the kind for talking."

"Shows you, it's hard to tell," Fargo said mildly. "I'll pay for the talk."

"If you pay, you can just sit and look at her all night, so far as I care." The woman half-shrugged. "Anyone in particular?"

"One of the Mexican girls, the one who gets the most play," Fargo said.

"That'd be Oleana," the woman said. "You're lucky. She's not busy at the moment."

Fargo watched as the woman lifted a heavy arm with bracelets and motioned to a girl sitting at a corner table. The girl rose at once, started toward him. She had dyed blond hair over a flat, wide peasant face with olive skin and dark eyes. It made her look a little like a tree with the wrong fruit on it, a plum tree with lemons, Fargo commented silently.

"The gentleman wants to talk to you," the woman said, unable to keep a smirk out of her voice.

The girl flashed more than the usual stock smile as she took in the intense handsomeness of the big black-haired man. She took his arm and led him upstairs to the first room in a dim hallway. He followed her into a small, cramped room, hardly large enough for more than the big bed and one chair. Fargo watched as she began to unbutton the tight bodice of her dress and the olive-skinned breasts began to tumble free, losing some of their shapeliness as they did so. Fargo put his hand over hers.

"Sit down. I said talk and that's what I want," he told her.

The girl eyed him a little suspiciously as she lowered

herself onto the edge of the bed. "What kind of talk?" she asked.

"Information," Fargo said. "You know of a man named Vilas?"

She hesitated a moment, then answered. "I know him," she said a little truculently.

"Tell me about him," Fargo said.

"Very handsome, *un hombre hermoso*. And very bad."

"You know his two friends?"

She shook her head. "I have only seen them." She made a face of disgust.

"But you have been with Vilas. He has come here to you," Fargo said, and the girl nodded. The Trailsman made a silent comment to himself. Vilas had done more than "pass through" Condor as Fern had said. He was known here, spent time here.

"Sometimes men talk after they've been with a woman. Did Vilas talk to you about himself?" Fargo asked.

She thought for a moment. "Once," she said.

"Once what?"

"Once he talk of his home."

"Did he say where?"

"In La Cruzada."

Fargo's eyes squinted in thought. "La Cruzada, that's inside the Mexican border, way south near Del Río." The girl shrugged and he returned his attention to her. "You know a man named Antonez?" he questioned.

"He never come to me, but I know him," she said, suddenly annoyed. "I wouldn't have him. A *Borracho, piojo indecente*."

Fargo nodded as his lips pursed. Antonez was a drunk and a shiftless, stupid lout, the girl had said. He saw her hand come up to rest against his chest. "Enough talk of these things. Something better now," she murmured.

Fargo took the bill from his pocket and pressed it into her hand. "*Gracias, señorita,*" he said, and half-smiled at the disappointment in her eyes. Compliments came in unexpected ways, sometimes. He left, went downstairs and through the noise and brightness of the main room of the dance hall, the madam watching him with curiosity as he left.

He walked the pinto to the stable and then went to the hotel room, undressed, and lay down on the lumpy mattress. He stayed awake for a moment and thought about a fancy saddle and one man already dead because of it. There'd be more, he was certain, because it was more than a fancy saddle. But before it was over, he'd know the truth, about fancy saddles and strawberry blondes that lied, and he'd be riding them both.

3

Fargo cantered up to the little house off Mesa Road exactly at noon, the sun hot and high, his lake-blue eyes taking in the group gathered outside with one long, sweeping glance. The lieutenant, dismounted, had brought his troop with him, ten of them, and Fargo saw Fern detach herself from the others, come toward him. He swung from the saddle as Fern reached him, her hair shining bright under the sun, a deep-red shirt, unbuttoned at the neck, curling tight around the undersides of her breasts. She held her face composed, but he caught the searching in her eyes as she looked at him.

"Did you find your cold bottle and warm woman last night?" she asked quietly, a hint of condescension in her voice.

"Didn't try," he said. "But I'm glad you're so concerned about me being happy. Now all you've got to do is work harder at it."

A little veil dropped over her eyes as she turned, walked beside him as he strode to the army troop, halted before the lieutenant. He focused on the men first, grunted in amazement and dismay, all apple-cheeked, unlined faces like the sergeant that had first come to him, all of them hardly more than boys. His glance went to the lieutenant, somewhat older, short blond hair, boyishly handsome, a face full of personal arrogance and officer-school conceit.

"Lieutenant Henry Vander," the man said, his voice as crisp as his pressed uniform.

Fargo let his eyes go back to the troopers on their horses. "They old enough to be out alone?" he murmured.

The lieutenant's face took on instant defensiveness. "I assure you, these troopers may be young but they're very capable. I've seen to that," he said stiffly.

Fargo's silence was a comment, and he shifted his glance to the two men sitting astride almost identical dark bays. Both were stern-faced, one balding, the other with carefully combed brown hair, both wearing suit jackets with their riding britches, both with dark stetsons hanging from their saddles.

"Frank Herbst," the one said. "First Southern Bank."

"Ronald Crane," the other added.

Fargo glanced at Robert Boswell, who stood watching, returned his glance to the lieutenant. "You first," he bit out. "How does the army fit into chasing after a fancy saddle?"

Vander cleared his throat. "Antonez, the man who first stole the saddle from Miss Blake's father, had hold of some very important government documents. We're certain they are in that saddle and we must get them back."

Fargo's glance moved to the two men from the bank, the question in the cold shale of his eyes. Herbst became the spokesman. "Vilas and his two friends robbed the First Southern Bank of a large amount of money. He hasn't had time to spend it and we're damn certain it's being carried in that saddle. We were sent to get it back," the man said.

Fargo heard Robert Boswell's voice cut in, turned to the man. "So, you see, everyone has their reason for get-

17

ting hold of that saddle, if not Vilas and his two cohorts," he said. "Now, are you going to accept our offer?"

"On one condition. We do things my way," Fargo said.

"Of course," Boswell said with a smile.

"Within reason," Lieutenant Vander added. "I can't have a civilian making army decisions. I'm sure you understand that, Fargo."

"I understand that what I say goes," Fargo returned, heard Boswell interrupt quickly.

"We've hired you for your abilities. I'm sure there'll be no conflicts," the man said. He was trying to be placating, and Fargo decided not to push any harder at the moment.

"If there's any kind of trouble, you'll find these troopers to be first-class, even if they are young," Vander said. He was high on pompous pride, Fargo grunted. Hell, he'd nothing else going for him.

"We leave in the morning. That'll give everyone a chance to get their gear together," Fargo said.

"I can leave this afternoon," Boswell said.

"Tomorrow morning," Fargo repeated firmly, swept the others with a glance. "You said you'd a few leads on Vilas. Let's have them."

"He passed through Condor," Fern said. "People saw him with the saddle, so we know he has it."

Fargo grunted, decided not to say he knew that Vilas had done more than pass through Condor. "Anything else?" he asked.

"We also know he told a few people he was heading south along the border," the other man from the bank offered.

"And we've heard that he was seen moving along the border country with his two friends and two pack-

18

horses," the man said. "That'd make five horses in all, enough to track, I'd say."

"That depends," Fargo said, let his lips purse. The border was an uncertain line, still subject to claims and counterclaims between Mexico, the United States, and the independent territory of Texas. The Rio Grande snaked its way along parts of it, behind the rock hills, which were a refuge for every kind of varmint, two- and four-legged. "Tomorrow morning, just after dawn. We'll meet here," he said to the others. He watched Lieutenant Vander turn to Fern, his eyes admiring.

"It'll be a pleasure riding with you, Miss Blake," the lieutenant said.

"Please call me Fern," the girl said, bestowing a smile made of archness, and Vander fairly glowed. He saluted, mounted his horse, and set off with his ten boy-troopers. Fargo saw Fern Blake glance at him, slightly smug.

"You pour on a lot of sugar when you want to," he commented blandly.

She drew instant protest into her eyes. "I was merely being polite. Lieutenant Vander is a gentleman," she snapped.

"And you figure to make him dance to your tune." Fargo laughed. "Tell me about this saddle. I want to know what it looks like."

She let go of her glare, let a deep breath escape her. "It's made of the finest hand-rubbed leather, stained a gunmetal gray," she began. "The cantle is bordered with silver inlay. A swelled fork is faced with silver and the horn is covered with stamped silver. The *tapaderos* are made of the finest bull-hide leather and the *rosaderos* made of calfskin rubbed and treated with buffalo oil. The jockeys are elkhide thongs with silver ring holes. The saddle itself is completely leather-embroidered in acanthus-leaf designs. The cinch rings are polished brass and the saddle is bordered with fancy stitching. Every piece is a perfect fit."

"It's a masterpiece of workmanship, I can tell you that," Boswell interjected.

"Should be easy enough to spot," Fargo said as he swung onto the pinto. "See you just after dawn tomorrow," he said, gave Fern a quick glance that held laughter in it. Damn, she was a pretty little package, he muttered silently as she half-glowered back at him, quick to catch the barb in his silent laugh. He rode on slowly, headed back toward Condor, stopped at a stream to let the pinto drink, cool off his ankles, and generally enjoy himself. Fargo leaned back against a tree. He'd heard all their stories, now, and he half-laughed aloud. He'd been right. They were all handing out phony reasons for the search. Fern and Boswell had come up with the fanciest. Also the hollowest. If Boswell had insisted on the saddle or his money back, Fern's father could have made some kind of trade-off for the stolen saddle. The man was supposed to be a saddlemaker. He had to have other fancy saddles on hand, enough for some kind of trade-off, maybe two for one. But instead, he sends his daughter out chasing a killer. It didn't make any sense. Fargo grunted derisively. It didn't make sense because it was a crock of shit.

Now the lieutenant's story, that was a simpler piece of fiction, Fargo reflected. But no less a crock of shit. Antonez had some important documents the army had to get back, Fargo echoed in his mind. Only . . . what was Antonez, a known drunk and a shiftless lout, doing with important army documents? Fargo smiled as he thought of how he'd almost tossed that one at the lieutenant but decided against it. Vander would only have fallen back on some weak answer, and it was best they all believed he had swallowed their stories.

The two men from the bank had the most straightforward tale, but that didn't hold up, either. Banks that were robbed usually sent out a reward if the amount was worth it, offered to anyone who brought in the culprits, or they left it to lawmen to handle. But suddenly this First Southern Bank sends out two special agents to chase down Vilas and his pals. Fargo grunted. Special agents because there were special reasons involved here. This wasn't any ordinary bank holdup. Fargo paused in his thoughts, frowned. Maybe there hadn't been any holdup at all. That part could be as phony as the rest.

He pushed himself up and swung onto the pinto. There were a few more items to pin down, and he rode back to town as the afternoon sun began to lower, came to a halt before the dance hall. It was a dim and empty place, the tables stood on end as an old man swept the floor. The big woman looked up from a corner of the long bar as he entered. "You again?" she questioned. "You're too early. We open at six."

"Where's Oleana?" Fargo said.

"Still asleep," the madam said.

"Wake her up," Fargo barked.

"More talk?" the woman asked, and he nodded. "You going to pay again?" she added, and Fargo nodded once more. "Then go wake her up yourself. You know her room," the woman said.

Fargo took the steps two at a time, opened the door of the first room at the top, and went inside. The girl was sprawled across the bed in a filmy nightgown in the dimness of the room, the shade drawn on the window. The yellow hair looked even more fake as she slept without her heavy makeup. He went to the bed, shook her gently. Her eyes opened slowly, dazed, finally focusing, and she pushed herself up to a sitting position. Her breasts fell free of the low-necked, filmy nightgown, large but nearing flabbiness. Without makeup she

21

looked not only older but worn. She frowned up at him as she gathered wakefulness.

"A few more questions," Fargo said.

She took on truculence. "I tell you all I know. I want to sleep some more," she said, started to lie back on the bed.

Fargo's hand shot out, yanked her up sharply. "Talk. You never earned a buck this easy. Where was Antonez killed? In Condor?" She nodded through her glower. "Where?"

She continued to glower at him. "Behind the feed store."

"Why did Vilas kill him?" Fargo asked.

"I don't know." She shrugged. "I hear they have fight."

"Over what?"

"Antonez always pick fights when he too drunk," she said.

"Did he have any friends?"

"Descanto, another *borracho*," she spit.

"Where can I find him?"

"The old house behind the feed store. Antonez lived there, too," she said.

Fargo tossed a crumpled bill at her and she closed her hand around it, was lying down again before he closed the door behind him. She must have had a heavy night after he'd left her, he mused as he hurried downstairs and outside into the gathering dusk. He found the feed store at the far end of the main street, circled behind it to an old house, hardly more than four walls leaning on each other. He pushed his way inside, smelled the man before he found him, the smell of cheap whiskey filling the tumbledown rooms, mingled with stale air and a musty, dank odor. Descanto, looking like a pile of old laundry, lay in a corner of the second room.

The man made muttering sounds as Fargo pulled him

22

up to a sitting position, caught him as he started to fall sideways at once. Fargo thought for a moment. It'd take a gallon of coffee and hours to bring him around that way. He reached down again, took the man's arm, and began to drag him across the rooms behind him. Descanto muttered again as Fargo dragged him outside, continued to drag him along the ground to one of the watering troughs. He lifted the man, tossed him into the trough, let him sink under, then pulled his head up by the greasy black hair. Descanto sputtered, blew water out of his mouth, and Fargo plunged him under again, pulled him up after a moment. Descanto's sputtering grew stronger. Fargo plunged him under the water six times and finally Descanto was gasping, protesting, half-sober.

Fargo held him by the hair, stared at the man's sunken face, his drained, yellowed, jaundiced skin. He started to plunge him under again. "No, no," the man said, coughing, and Fargo grunted, pulled him from the trough to let him lay gasping on the ground. The entire scene had drawn only a few curious glances from those passing. Descanto lifted his head, stared up at the big, black-haired man. "¡Caramba, hombre! ¿Qué pasa?" he muttered, fear in his eyes.

"You sober enough to listen?" Fargo growled. The man shook his head. "Tell me about Antonez," Fargo said.

"He is dead," Descanto said.

"I know that and I know who killed him. What did they fight about?" Fargo questioned.

"Antonez sell Vilas a saddle for a bottle of rum. Then he try to steal it back. Vilas kill him," the man said, pulling himself to his feet.

"Antonez ever do any work for the soldiers, the United States army?" Fargo questioned.

Descanto made a derisive sound. "Antonez work for the soldiers? You make joke, *Hombre*," he said.

"No jokes. Did he ever run any errands · for the army?" Fargo pressed.

"Antonez would not go near soldiers. Once, long time ago, he steal an army horse. They catch him, put him in jail a long time. He stay far away from soldiers," the man said.

Fargo grunted. He had all the answers he wanted for the moment. He tossed a coin at Descanto, enough for him to buy a new bottle of rot-gut, and walked away as the man scrambled for it. So Antonez never went near soldiers, Fargo echoed as he walked the pinto back toward the hotel room. The good Lieutenant Vander's story was phony. Antonez never had any important army documents in his hands. Nor was he a clever operator and con artist as Fern and Boswell had tried to portray him. He was a drunk and a petty thief, nothing more. Vilas, knowing a fine saddle when he saw it, was happy to make the trade.

Fargo stabled the pinto, returned to his room at the hotel to stretch out on the bed as night settled over the town. A few items were taking definite shape. He'd been lied to, but then, he'd been pretty certain of that. Now it had been confirmed. He let his thoughts drift on of themselves. Vilas probably didn't know the saddle was so important to so many people, Fargo reflected. It was just a fine saddle to him, worth owning and riding. Only it was more, a lot more. But why? What was so damn important about a fancy saddle? What could make such a strange parley—one very pretty girl, her companion, two bank agents, and the United States army—all want their hands on one saddle?

Each one had come up with a story that tied in with the basic facts: Antonez had stolen the saddle and Vilas had taken it from him. But each had invented their own lie for the rest. They'd put their heads together to hire him, yet why did he have the feeling that if he got them within smelling distance of the saddle they'd fall out like thieves? He half-chuckled to himself. Instinct, that sixth sense he'd long ago learned to trust. They invented their own stories and they each had their own reasons for wanting the saddle. He'd make a bet on that much.

Fargo pushed himself from the bed. There was no percentage in guessing further about it now. He'd find out the answers on the trail, either before or after he got his hands on that saddle. He stretched, went downstairs, and walked outside into the night. Only a few doors from the dance hall a man named Higgens ran a late-night eatery, getting much of his business from stragglers who wandered into Condor at all hours. It was a rundown place, but Higgens furnished an edible piece of steak and his coffee was always fresh. Fargo sat down in a corner, washed the food down with two cups of coffee, and watched a man and a woman eat their meal without a single word between them. He relaxed, exchanged small talk with Higgens, and finally strolled back to the hotel. He walked up the half-darkened steps to his room, neared it, and suddenly halted, his body tensing with the instant reaction of a mountain lion. He was up on the balls of his feet as his hand went to the butt of the Colt .45 in the holster at his hip. The little flicker of light from the bottom crack of the closed door to the room would have gone unnoticed by most people.

Fargo drew the Colt from the holster as his hand swallowed the doorknob. Slowly, silently, he eased the door open and caught the light as it flickered again, a candle inside. He pushed the door open farther, enough to see the figure, crouched over his saddlebag, back to him, a flat-brimmed Mexican hat covering the back of its head. The figure lifted the candle higher to see into the pockets of the saddlebag. Fargo took a single, long step into the room, moving almost halfway across it on silent cat's feet. He pushed the barrel of the Colt into the back of the crouched figure.

"Hold it right there," he growled, felt the figure stiffen. "Now turn, slow and easy," he said. The figure turned carefully, straightened up to face him. "I'll be damned." Fargo frowned, taking in the girl in front of him. He reached over, turned the lamp on, and the soft yellow light of the kerosene lamp slowly illuminated the room. Fargo stared at the girl, a young, almost beautiful face with a straight nose, full lips, and eyes that were vibrant pools of blackness. Jet hair hung down loosely from her face, a face that carried just enough of a hint of flat cheekbones and strong bone structure under the bronze-olive skin to whisper Indian blood somewhere behind her. She wore a gray shirt and full, high breasts pressed it tight across her chest. A small waist widened to full hips under a black riding skirt.

"What the hell are you?" Fargo growled.

"Carlita," the girl said. "Carlita Orez." The vibrant black eyes met his boldly.

"That doesn't tell me why the hell you're in my room," Fargo muttered.

"You are the one they hired to find Vilas?" she returned.

"I'm asking the questions," Fargo snapped. "What were you doing going through my saddlebag?"

"To see if you are the one they call the Trailsman," she said.

"I am," Fargo said.

"Then you are the one they hire to find Vilas and the saddle he stole," the girl said.

"Jesus, you after that saddle, too?" Fargo blurted out.

"I don't care about any saddle," the girl said, and Fargo let his eyes move over her again. Almost beautiful, he repeated silently, a throbbing vibrancy in her.

"Then what are you doing here in my room?" he asked.

"I want to go with you. I can find Vilas for you," she said.

"I can find him for myself," Fargo answered.

"Not so quick as with me," the girl said. "I know him well. I know what he would do and what he would not do and I know the border mountains." She flicked a glance at the big Colt still in Fargo's hand. "Can you put that away, please?" she said, blowing out the candle she held.

Fargo's eyes stayed on her as he holstered the gun. "Carlita Orez," he said slowly. "You Mexican?"

"Half," she answered. "And half French."

"Maybe a little Indian, too?" he offered, and she half-shrugged. "Why do you want to help me find Vilas?" Fargo asked.

"Because I want to find him, too," she answered.

"Why?"

"So I can kill him," she flung back.

"That's sure enough a good reason," Fargo remarked mildly. "Why do you want to do that?"

"He was to make me his woman. Everyone knew that. But he ran off and left me. You know what that means here, on the border, among my people?" she blazed.

"I've an idea." Fargo nodded.

The black eyes flashed. "It means disgrace. It means he laughed at me, spit on me. It means I'll always be known as the woman Vilas threw away. I'll have respect again only by paying him for it, by killing him."

Fargo's eyes stayed on the beauty of her bronze-olive face, made more so by the flush of color that had come into it, the passion inside her exploding. She didn't lie about the ancient codes down here. He knew that much. A woman cast aside became an object of ridicule and scorn. A whore fared better. Unjust, unreasonable, cruel

27

codes, yet as immovable as the sandstone mountains. At least she didn't gave a damn about the saddle, Fargo grunted silently, a refreshing change.

"How'd you hear about their hiring me?" he asked.

"Words have feet," she said. "They travel quickly. The soldiers talk easily at the dance hall. I was told about it."

Damn, Fargo swore under his breath, and felt the anger pull at him. Loose talk always carried trouble. He swore again, returned his attention to the girl. He watched the deep black eyes grow less angry and she took a step toward him.

"It will be a long, hard journey. Take me and I will make the time better for you," she said.

He searched her face, the meaning in her words clear enough. She met his eyes boldly, her head held high. "What if I want a sample first, now?" He grinned at her.

The black fire flashed in her eyes instantly. "No. I am no dance-hall *puta*," she snapped. "Take me with you and I will keep my word." Her hand went to the top button of the gray shirt. She flipped it open, then the next, and the bronze-olive curve of her breasts swelled into the open. She pulled the blouse open and he could see half of each full, deep breast, the edge of one dark-brown areola peeking out from the line of the shirt. "Am I not beautiful enough for that alone?" she asked.

Fargo chuckled. She knew how to use her weapons, how to pressure. "You're beautiful enough, Carlita Orez," he said, "Beautiful as all hell."

"Then take me with you. I can help you find him," she said quickly, pulling the shirt back in place.

"You really think you can do that?" Fargo asked.

"I know I can. I know that *zoquete*," she spit out. "I know how he thinks, how he moves, how he laughs, and how he kills."

28

"Why didn't you know he'd walk out on you?" Fargo tossed at her.

Her full red lips pressed down onto each other before she answered. "I should have known. Sometimes you don't see what you do not want to see," she said simply.

Fargo half-smiled at the answer. Wisdom had little to do with book-learning. Fargo let his thoughts race on for a moment. It promised to be an interesting search. Why not make it more so? Besides, he'd welcome any help in finding Vilas for himself.

"If I say yes, Carlita, you give your advice to me, no-body else. Do you *comprende*?" he said.

"*Sí*," she answered, and a tiny smile touched her lips to make the beauty of her suddenly more alive. Her eyes moved up and down his long, hard-muscled frame. "They did not tell me you were so *guapo*," she said, using the street tongue for good-looking.

"Maybe I'm mean, too," Fargo said.

She studied him again. "No, not mean. *Duro*, hard, and *peligroso*. I would not want you for an enemy. But not mean, not the way you say it."

He laughed. "We leave tomorrow morning, Carlita Orez," he said, and her tiny smile exploded into a short, happy gasp. Her arms went around him and her lips pressed his mouth, soft lips, very soft skin, and she let her tongue flicker across his mouth and then stepped back.

"*Gracias*. You will not be sorry, *amigo*," she said.

"I don't figure to be," Fargo said. "I am called Fargo." She nodded, her eyes continuing to examine him with unmasked appreciation. "There is a house off Mesa Road," he said.

"I know it. Old Man Ryan rents it out," she said.

"Meet me there, just after dawn breaks," Fargo told her, and she nodded. "Where do you live now?"

"At the end of town, with old friends," she said. "I'll be there in the morning, ready to go." She flashed a quick smile as she paused at the door, a smile made of satisfaction and of promise, and he watched the door close behind her. He waited, gave her time to get downstairs and outside, then moved with pantherlike quick grace, long, crouching strides, and reached the street outside in time to see her moving off into the darkness. He started to follow, ducked against the side of the hotel as he glimpsed the figure detach itself from the deep shadows and follow after her. Fargo moved carefully, his eyes on the figure, a man, medium height, thin, wearing a small-brimmed sombrero. The man followed Carlita, staying a distance back, and Fargo stayed behind him as the girl walked on until she reached almost the last house in Condor, a white stucco square house.

The man following her halted, pressed himself into the deeper shadows and Fargo did the same. Carlita went into the house and Fargo watched as the man waited, finally turned, and started back down the street. Fargo stayed in the blackness near a wooden structure, watched the figure go by, turn into a narrow side alley. Fargo followed until the man entered a house and, moments later, a window glowed with lamplight. Fargo started to retrace his steps to the hotel, his eyes narrowed in thought. Someone else was very interested in Carlita Orez. The man had made no move toward her, had been content just to watch where she went and follow. A silent admirer? A rejected suitor? The girl was beautiful enough to have many tongues panting for her. Or was the man keeping watch on her for other reasons? Was he waiting to see if she were going off alone?

Fargo reached the hotel, shook aside further speculation. It was pointless, and he went to the room, undressed, and fell onto the bed. Carlita's appearance and her silent observer were just two more pieces in a strange puzzle that was taking on more pieces every time he turned around. He closed his eyes to sleep as his lips edged a tiny smile. He was beginning to look forward to this job.

4

The new sun was just caressing the tops of the jojoba bushes when Fargo rode up to the little house off Mesa Road. The lieutenant and his pink-cheeked troopers were lined up smartly and Fargo's eyes swept by them to where Fern stood beside a gray mare. She saw his eyes go over the horse. A short-legged, stocky mount, no speed in her but plenty of endurance. He let a tiny smile touch his lips. Fern figured to be ready for the kind of mountain riding that could hobble the average horse. Boswell nodded pleasantly as Fargo glanced at him. Herbst and Crane sat two almost identical bay horses and Fargo passed his glance back to the lieutenant.

"How many others know about this little expedition?" Fargo muttered.

Vander's face took on a questioning frown. "I beg your pardon?" he said.

"Your boys have loose lips. They've been talking about chasing after a fancy saddle in the dance hall," Fargo bit out.

"I don't believe that," Vander protested.

"I don't give a damn whether you believe it or not. I'm only wondering who else is getting ideas about it, what with the army chasing after it," Fargo said.

"I'm sure you won't have to concern yourself with anyone else," Vander said stiffly.

"You're sure? That makes me feel a lot better," Fargo said, making no effort to hide the sarcasm in his voice. The lieutenant's eyes hardened as Fern's voice cut in.

"I suggest the best thing is to get moving," she said, and Fargo met her eyes. They echoed the touch of haughty imperiousness in her tone.

"Soon," Fargo said.

Her frown was instant. "Why soon? Everyone's ready and waiting."

Fargo was about to answer when Carlita came into view, cantering up, jet-black hair blowing in the wind, her bronze-olive skin set off against a white-cotton blouse under which her breasts swayed beautifully. She came to a halt looking vibrantly beautiful, flashed a wide smile. "Good morning, Fargo," she said. "I am ready."

He returned the smile, watched her move her black-eyed glance across the others as she sat on the solid chestnut gelding. "*Buenos días, amigos*," she said.

"This is Carlita Orez," Fargo introduced. "She's going with us," he added blandly.

"What?" It was Herbst who barked the word.

"She's going with us," Fargo repeated.

"I don't understand," Boswell remarked.

Fern's voice, tight, cut in. "I do," she snapped.

Fargo looked at her, a half-smile on his lips. "Carlita is going to help me find Vilas for you," he said.

"I'm afraid taking anyone else is out of the question," Vander said. "This is official army business, after all."

"You want that saddle?" Fargo asked pleasantly.

"Of course," Vander said.

"Then Carlita goes along." Fargo smiled.

"What makes you think this young woman can help you track Vilas?" Boswell questioned.

"She knows a lot about him and that'll be a real help," Fargo said.

"This is highly irregular." Vander frowned.

Fargo fastened him with a harsh glance, let his eyes sweep the others. "You hired me to get that saddle for you. How I do it is up to me. Whether I use a cross-eyed lynx, a witch-hazel wand, or a beautiful girl is my business," he said curtly. He let his glance come to rest on Fern, saw her eyes shooting spears of blue fury at him. "You've anything to say?" he asked.

"Plenty, but I'd rather say it in private," she snapped. "May I see you alone for a moment?" She turned, not waiting for an answer, strode around the side of the house.

He slid from the saddle, followed her around to the other side of the house, and she spun around to face him. "Dammit, Fargo, I know why you're taking that girl along," she hissed.

"I told you, because she can help me find Vilas and your fancy saddle," he said mildly.

"*Hah!*" she barked. "Maybe the others will swallow that, but I know better. You wanted a warm woman and a cold bottle, but the money we've offered is appealing, so you're trying to have both. You're bringing her so you can enjoy your lusting, so you can have your cake and eat it."

"My, you put it so crudely, Fern, honey." Fargo smiled.

The color rose from her graceful neck to flood her cheeks. "That was a figure of speech," she said.

"Oh." Fargo smiled. "Anyway, you're all wrong."

"Like hell I am, and I can prove that," Fern snapped.

Fargo's eyes lifted in interest. "How?"

"What if I said I'd be her stand-in? You'd send her packing at once."

"You offering?" Fargo asked.

"I'm just making a point. Go on, tell me you wouldn't," Fern pressed.

"You offer and I'll tell you," Fargo said casually.

"You're disgraceful. She can't be over seventeen," Fern blazed.

"Women down here are like *chilitipine* peppers." Fargo shrugged, saw the tiny frown touch her brow. "They get ripe early and hot fast."

"You're oversexed," Fern accused.

"Rather be over than under, honey." He grinned and saw her hand move, start to come up, but she held back, her lips quivering.

"Bastard," she hissed. "You get rid of her at the first town we reach. You've been hired to work, not play." She whirled, spun away, and stalked off. Fargo strolled from behind the house, ignoring the others watching, climbed onto the pinto, and rode forward. Carlita fell in beside him and he looked back, saw Lieutenant Vander start off at the head of his line of troopers. Fern swung her horse beside him. Boswell, Herbst, and Crane rode at the rear. Fargo laughed as he watched Fern work hard to force a smile over the seething inside her as she concentrated on Vander, knew she heard his chuckle.

"She is made of high-toned ideas, that one," Carlita said to him. "And something else."

"Such as?" Fargo asked.

"She wants and she does not want to know it," Carlita said.

Fargo laughed at the woman's wisdom in her words, stepped up the pace as he led the way along the Texas-Mexican border, staying mostly on the Texas side. The rugged red-clay hills rose up and he hugged the base of them, where the chufa grew thick and fire thorns somehow managed to grow up into the rocks. He set a steady pace, watched the others behind him, and saw everyone keeping the pace well. Fern had stopped chattering with

Vander as the sun grew hotter, but she kept the tan sleeveless vest over her blouse. Carlita had opened the top buttons of her shirt and the bronze-olive breasts moved back and forth in carelessly beautiful rhythm.

Fargo called a halt to rest the horses in midafternoon when they came upon an almost dry creek with just enough water to cool hot hooves. Vander walked to him, gave Carlita a stiff bow. "No need to go slow to pick up a trail yet," Vander said.

"I wasn't," Fargo replied.

"Just head for Historia. Vilas was there," Vander said.

"In Historia?" Carlita frowned.

"That's right," the lieutenant said. "It's right on the border. My men can go there."

Fargo's eyes held on Carlita, saw the frown stay on her face. "How do you know he stopped at Historia?" Fargo asked the lieutenant.

"He was seen there," Vander answered.

"Who saw him?" Fargo questioned.

"A silver prospector who came to Condor."

"You couldn't check his story, of course," Fargo said, his glance flicking to Carlita.

"No, naturally not. But he said he'd seen a man riding a fancy saddle in Historia," Vander returned.

Carlita snapped the answer. "There are other fancy saddles. Vilas would not go to Historia," she said.

"Why?" Fargo asked, beating Vander to the question.

"It's not his kind of town," the girl said. "He does not like Mexican whores. That's all there is in Historia. He would not go there. He'd go to Tallowville, maybe, or Dry Bend, but not Historia."

"I'll go with what Carlita says," Fargo remarked.

Vander stiffened, instantly unwilling to accept Carlita's judgment over his own. "I've a positive lead," the lieutenant said.

"You've got nothing," Fargo crackled.

"I've a lead," Vander repeated. "Until you've something better I insist we follow through on it and go on to Historia."

"It'll waste a day," Fargo said.

"I think it will be most worthwhile," Vander returned, almost clicked his heels as he spun and strode off. Fern watched from nearby, Fargo saw, became aware of Carlita's eyes on him.

"It is not your decision to make?" the girl asked softly.

"It is, but I'm going to let the lieutenant have his way this time." Fargo smiled at her and the smile was edged with ice. Carlita's black eyes studied him and slowly he saw the corners of her mouth turn up.

"*Comprendo*," she said. "You will teach him by, how you call it, a lesson?"

"An object lesson," Fargo said, swinging one foot into the stirrups. "Let's ride."

He caught Fern's glance as they moved forward and she found a moment to come up alongside him as he nosed the pinto ahead of the others. "You agreed too easily back there," she slid at him, the blue eyes probing.

"Just being reasonable," he said. "I'm easy to get along with."

"Hell you are," Fern said. "You're up to something."

"So young and so suspicious," Fargo chided. She glared at him, turned her gray mare away as Carlita came up.

"She is more *lista*, more smart, than the others, that one," Carlita commented.

Fargo agreed in silence, kept a steady pace as dusk began to shoulder the day aside.

Historia took shape in the fading light, the edge of it in Texas, the rest sprawling across the border into Mexico. Carlita's description of the town had been accurate. It was mostly one big, ramshackle whorehouse with a row of yellow lights across the front of it, clearly visible from the edge of town where Vander halted the troop as Fargo raised a hand.

"We make camp first," Fargo said. He gestured to a flat circle up on a rise in the sandstone rocks, bordered on three sides by rocky formations. "Up there," he ordered, led the way without waiting for agreement from Vander. He dismounted when he reached the small area, and Carlita swung from her horse, her eyes picking out a spot to the right, at the edge of the circle and against a cluster of rock. She flicked her eyes to him, gestured, and he nodded, watched her start to carry her saddlebag to the spot. Herbst, Crane, and Boswell dismounted, and Fargo saw Fern stay on the gray mare, halting beside Vander.

"I don't think you'd best go into town, Miss Fern," Vander said. "It does seem a rather unsavory place."

Fern shot a glance at Fargo. He let only total unconcern show in his strong-featured, intense face. "Perhaps you're right," she agreed. "I'll start dinner if the gentlemen will get a fire going."

"At once," Boswell said.

"Ready?" Vander asked, and Fargo nodded. The lieutenant motioned his troop to start down from the rise toward Historia. Fargo swung the pinto beside him.

"You think we need all your troopers?" he asked mildly.

"A show of force helps to loosen people's tongues," the lieutenant said.

"Only in the army manual," Fargo commented as they rode into Historia. They passed a lone general store, closed for the night, a few weathered shacks, and halted before the long front of the whorehouse. A few scroungy characters moved in and out through the swinging doors and the row of yellow gaslights illuminated a paint-peeling sign that said:

"Vilas will have stopped here. He fancies himself quite a ladies' man, I'm told," the lieutenant said, dismounting. Carlita's comments stayed with him and Fargo made no reply. Vander ordered six of his troopers to go with him and marched into the whorehouse. Fargo followed, moving to one side, his lake-blue eyes hard as they swept the place in one glance. A towering woman, at least two hundred pounds, in a wraparound green skirt and a white blouse, occupied the center of the room, leaning against the long bar. The name, Mama Lupe, fitted her all too well. Her dark eyes glittered coldly, a wolflike, predatory quality in her large-nosed face with a red slit of a mouth. Mama Lupe spoke, a voice of brass that echoed the hardness of her.

"Well, now, step right in. Mama Lupe likes soldier boys here," the woman said, and her smile was devouring.

"This isn't that kind of visit, I'm afraid," Vander said with ridiculous formality in his voice.

Fargo's eyes went to the half-dozen or more girls watching from the back of the big room, all young, all full-figured in cheap, too-tight dresses, and all younger versions of Mama Lupe. He saw their eyes take in the young troopers the way a lynx looks at a rabbit. Three men, sallow-faced, squinty-eyed, all wearing guns, watched from each corner of the room, not as customers.

"Well, now, what kind of a visit is it, soldier?" Mama Lupe asked, the hard fixed smile pasted over her face.

"We want information. We're looking for a man named Vilas. We think he was here, with one of your girls," Vander said.

Mama Lupe's glance slowly moved around the room to the girls, lingering on each one for a moment, and each girl shrugged or shook her head. The woman's eyes returned to Vander; the girls continued to look at the troopers hungrily. "No, as you saw, Lieutenant, my girls don't know him. And they have good memories. When do you think he was here?"

"A few days ago, maybe a week at the most," Vander said.

"No, my girls would remember. But why don't you and your soldier boys stay awhile, relax here with us? You can always chase after this Vilas," the woman suggested with her devouring smile.

Fargo watched the troopers, saw the eagerness in their eyes.

"He's handsome, I'm told," Vander said.

"Nobody handsome been in here until now," the woman said, trying another smile, and her girls slid out a ripple of agreement. Fargo started out the door and saw Vander glance at him. He was on the pinto when the lieutenant emerged with his troopers, mounted his horse.

"They're no doubt lying," Vander said stiffly.

"All together? They rehearse for it?" Fargo said mildly.

"Mama Lupe gave them the sign and they took it from there," the lieutenant said.

"Vilas never came through here. Carlita said he wouldn't," Fargo answered.

"I'm not convinced of that at all," Vander said pompously as he led the way back to the campsite. When they reached it, Fargo wheeled the pinto to the side, unsaddled the horse, and glanced at the little fire where Fern dished out plates of hot beans. Carlita brought him one and he sat beside her at the edge of the circle. The tiny half-smile on her lips made telling her about Mama Lupe's unnecessary. Fern sat beside the fire with Vander, strawberry-blond hair gleaming in the light of the flames.

"My bedroll is behind the rocks up above," Carlita said, indicating a cluster of stones. Fargo nodded, rose to wash off his plate when he saw the apple-cheeked sergeant stop to talk to Vander. Fern left, paused beside him to scrape off her plate. Fargo saw the sergeant break into a wide grin and rush off to the other troopers. He felt the frown furrow his brow as they rose, started for their mounts.

"Vander, what the hell's going on?" Fargo barked.

The lieutenant turned to him. "My boys want to relax some and I agreed," he said with a hint of disdain.

"You letting them go back to Mama Lupe?" Fargo frowned.

"They pointed out this could be their last chance for some fun for a while. This could be a long search," Vander said. "I told them they had to be back by midnight. They'll be here. They're well-disciplined. I believe in keeping my troopers happy."

"Bullshit," Fargo barked. "You still figure they'll get one of those whores to talk about Vilas."

Vander looked slightly smug. "I did tell them to try and combine business with pleasure," he said.

Fargo's glance swept past Fern, listening from a few paces away, to the troopers as they rode single file from the campsite. "You better get them back right now," he said. "You're making one big mistake, mister."

"I know my boys. They'll be back at midnight and they've all been in whorehouses before," the lieutenant said.

"There are whores and whores," Fargo growled, turned, and walked off. Carlita's head peered down from the edge of the cluster of rocks above as he took down his bedroll. He caught the flash of red-blond hair out of the corner of his eye as Fern halted beside him.

"I've confidence in Lieutenant Vander's judgment," she said.

"So do I," Fargo said, and she eyed him warily. "I'm sure it's lousy," he finished, strode away. He put his bedroll down along the far side of the campsite, made his way up behind the cluster of rocks. He found Carlita sitting cross-legged on her bedroll, her skirt still on but her shirt off. The long, thick jet-black hair hung down over her breasts, allowing only a glimpse of softly curved flesh.

"We sleep alone tonight, Fargo," she said.

"That an opinion, a question, or a comment?" he said.

The black eyes caught a tiny twinkle of light. "A truth," she countered deftly. "You will want to be ready if these *infantas* don't come back."

She was right, of course, and he uttered a grunt of wry appreciation. "Boys playing at being men and a stupid-ass lieutenant. Trouble," he muttered, bent down, pressed his mouth on hers, a soft kiss, full of promise. "You're looking beautiful," he murmured.

Her full lips opened for his mouth, pushed gently, then drew back, and he straightened, started to turn just as a wisp of wind blew against one band of the thick black hair and he glimpsed the tip of a pink-brown nipple that was covered again at once. "Soon enough," he said.

"I can wait," she answered with a hint of laughter in her voice.

He hurried around the other side of the rocks and back to where he'd set out his bedroll. He took off only his boots, stretched out with his arms behind his head, squinted around the campsite. The fire out, only a half-moon outlined the others. Herbst and Crane had bedded down side by side with Boswell nearby. The lieutenant had spread his bedroll in prescribed cavalry fashion, the corners half-turned, ready to be rolled up in an instant. He caught the glimpse of strawberry-blond hair over the top edge of a blanket to his right, the shape beneath it indicating her back was to him. He closed his eyes, let tiredness sweep down to take command. He set the interior alarm clock he'd learned to operate long ago, and slept.

5

The half-moon was just starting to slide down the blue-velvet cloth of the sky when he woke, eyes open and alert at once. He picked out Vander's figure pacing back and forth on the far side of the campsite. Fargo pulled on boots, rose, and sauntered toward the man.

"How long past due are they?" he asked as Vander watched him approach with lips tightened. The lieutenant drew a pocket watch from inside his uniform trousers.

"Almost two hours," he said. "I don't understand it." He frowned. Fargo's face held irritated contempt. "Something's wrong. I'm going in," Vander said.

Fargo saw Boswell sitting up, watching, then Herbst and Crane woke, taking in the situation at a glance. A movement caught the corner of his eye and he saw Fern, standing, wrapped in a powder-blue cotton robe, her brow furrowed in concern.

"You can't go in alone," she said to Vander.

"I would appreciate some backup," the lieutenant said.

"I'll ride with you. Herbst, you come along. Boswell and Crane stay here," Fargo said, started for the pinto. He was just tightening the cinch under the horse's belly when Fern came to him.

"I appreciate your going with Lieutenant Vander," she said. "That was nice of you."

"Don't get carried away. I'd let him stew in his own juice, but his soldier boys might come in handy before this is over," Fargo told her coldly, and her lips tightened.

"My apologies," she snapped. "Don't you ever do anything because it's the proper thing to do?"

"Damn seldom," he said, swung onto the pinto, and watched her stalk away. He wheeled the horse to follow Vander, waved a hand at Carlita as she peered down from behind the rocks. Herbst drew alongside him and they rode in silence for the few minutes it took to reach Historia. The town was deserted, Mama Lupe's silent, the row of yellow gaslights turned off. The ten horses were still tied up outside and Vander frowned as he swung to the ground, started in through the two swinging doors of the whorehouse. The big Colt .45 was in Fargo's hand as he moved after the lieutenant. Vander drew on his own army-issue Colt as he entered the silent, dark room. He groped along the wall till he found a lamp, turned the gas knob on, and the room began to take on a dim, yellow light.

Fargo saw the lieutenant's jaw drop open in shock. His troopers were there, three still slumped over the tables, the other seven sprawled on the floor, each one stark naked. "My God," Vander gasped.

Fargo reached the first naked body in one long stride, knelt down beside it. "Are they dead?" he heard Vander choke out.

"Not likely," Fargo muttered. "They're whoring thieves, not killers, 'less you force their hand." He leaned down to the young boy's face. "Drugged solid," he said grimly. "They were slipped knockout drops."

Vander, shock still gripping his face, glanced around

the room. "Everything's gone, their clothes, boots, guns," he gasped.

"Money, rings, watches, you name it and it's gone," Fargo added, straightening up. "They cleaned 'em out real good."

"Those rotten, thieving bitches," Vander said, his voice taking on its usual pompousness as he recovered from his initial shock. He started to lift one naked trooper, let the limp form slide back to the floor. "My God, what do we do now?" he muttered.

"Bring them around," Fargo said.

"How?"

"There's probably some coffee around here someplace. Make a big pot of it, pour it into them. Coffee, then douse them with water, more coffee and more water. Figure on all night to get them on their feet," Fargo said.

"I'll find the coffee," Herbst said.

Fargo moved back as the man started into a back room and Vander began to rummage through the rear of the bar. Fargo slipped outside silently, paused for a moment, moved around to the rear of the old frame building. He crouched down in front of the rear door, his eyes on the wagon tracks, easy to spot even in the light of the half-moon. One wagon, three horses with it, he noted. He swung onto the pinto and began to follow the tracks that led out of the other end of the excuse for a town that was Historia and up into a hillside of scruffy condalia.

He followed the trail, not hurrying and not surprised by how far they'd gone as he moved along the low hillside of rock and brush. Mama Lupe and her girls had done it before, he was certain. They had it down to a routine, knew exactly what to expect. Most times their victims, when they came to, were too embarrassed to do more than slink away. Mama Lupe and her whores would just lay low until it was safe to return and sell off whatever they'd taken that was worth selling. This time

46

they'd hit the jackpot. Army boots, guns, hard-wearing uniform trousers, all would bring good money, to say nothing of rings and watches and whatever cash the troopers had on them. A chicken-shit operation but effective enough, Fargo grunted as he continued to climb through the hillside.

He suddenly slowed as, beyond a high rock, he espied the house, a dark silhouette of a ramshackle frame structure, halfway between a shack and a house. The wagon was pulled up along the side, a long-sided Texas hauling wagon with four arched top bows. Fargo slid noiselessly from the saddle, moved on foot toward the house, his eyes blue shale as they scanned the area. Mama Lupe felt so confident she hadn't posted a guard, and he spotted the three other horses tied up at a corner of the house. He heard the sound of high-pitched laughter from inside the house as he moved toward a window. Flattening himself against the house, he edged closer to the square of yellow light, carefully peered in through the window, his jaw muscles tensing as he took in the scene.

The girls were sitting on the floor, the troopers' things heaped high in a pile. The girls were separating their booty: uniform jackets in one pile, trousers in another, guns in a small heap, boots in still another, rings and watches in a little mound to one side. Mama Lupe sat on a high stool against one wall and the three sallow-faced characters he'd seen at the whorehouse were taking turns at a bottle of whiskey.

Fargo pulled his head back, moved on silent steps to the door of the house and stepped behind it. He knelt down, picked up a loose rock, and sent it clattering noisily across the ground.

Mama Lupe's hard voice barked at once. "What the hell was that?"

"Kangaroo rats," Fargo heard one of the men answer.

47

"Take a look. There's food in the wagon," he heard Mama Lupe order.

Fargo lifted himself onto the balls of his feet, the big Colt in his hand as he heard the figure come to the door, pull it open, and step outside. The man peered across the darkness, took a step away from the house and toward the wagon. Fargo pressed the barrel of the Colt into the back of his neck.

"One sound and your head goes off," he whispered. The man stiffened and Fargo pressed the gun harder against his neck. "Walk, nice and slow, over to those rocks," he breathed. The man began to move forward and Fargo went with him, keeping the gun against the back of his neck. Reaching the line of low rocks, he pushed the man to his knees with his other hand, took the gun from his holster, and tossed it away. "You won't be needing it," he told the man.

"Whatever you doing, *amigo*, you're a dead man," the sallow-faced one hissed.

Fargo jammed the gun harder into the man's neck. "Shut up or you'll be deader faster," he growled. He waited, crouched, the moments like hours until the door of the house opened again. A second man emerged, squinted into the night.

"Tomás," he called. "Where are you?"

Fargo kept the gun against the back of the man's neck as the other one stepped forward, peered to his right, then his left. Fargo waited, let him move further from the doorway.

"*¿Qué pasa?*" the man called out.

Fargo put his other hand halfway around the man's neck as he lifted the barrel of the Colt away, took aim at the thin figure outside the house. His finger pressed upon the trigger, starting to draw it back when he felt the neck in his grip twist, tear away. "*¡Cuidado!*" the man screamed.

"Shit," Fargo swore. "Goddamn stupid bastard." He leveled the Colt at the diving figure trying to scramble away, then snapped the gun up as the other man went into a half-crouch and yanked his gun out. Fargo fired, a single shot. It smashed into the man's chest and he saw the half-crouched figure seem to blow away, sailing back, arms flung outward. Fargo whirled again at the first man, saw the figure diving toward him, an eight-inch skinning knife in his hand. The blade ripped upward at his belly as the man came in low, lips pulled back in fury.

There was no chance for a shot as Fargo twisted to the side, felt the knifeblade nick the edge of his gun belt. He landed on his side, spun around, but the wiry, lithe figure was lightning fast, coming at him instantly with the wicked blade slicing the air. Fargo rolled again as the blade almost caught him across the shoulder, kept rolling, half-turned, and fired a shot that grazed the man's shoulder. It slowed him a fraction and he stumbled, enough time for Fargo to bring the Colt up properly. The man sprang at him and he fired directly at the diving figure. The sallow face exploded in an explosion of bone and blood. The faceless form hurtled past him to bury itself between two rocks.

"Stupid bastard," Fargo said again through tight lips. He heard the high-pitched shouts from inside the house, leaped to his feet, and saw the third man start to emerge, gun in hand. "Hold it there," he called out. The man half-turned, fired two shots, both wide, then dived back into the house, where more excited shouts sounded. Fargo moved silently along the line of the rocks, crept behind a spread of the piny condalia bushes, and moved to where the three extra horses were tethered. He dropped to one knee, the Colt raised, ready to fire. He drew a deep breath and waited. It was not a long wait. The figure came around from the other side of the house in a crouch, having gone out through another window. He made for the horses and Fargo saw him jam a foot into the stirrup of the nearest horse, shake the reins loose, and swing onto the saddle.

"That horse moves and you're a dead man," Fargo called out, his voice cold and flat. "Be smarter than your friends." He saw the man's feet push out, come in hard against the horse's ribs. Fargo had the Colt up as the horse started to bolt forward. He fired one shot and the rider rose half-out of the saddle, his body arching backward. He flew off in a converse arc as the horse raced on and his head hit the ground first, the rest of his body coming up and over in a backward somersault. Fargo heard the sharp crack of his neck as it broke. The figure lay absolutely still, facedown, and Fargo rose, stepped across the open space toward the house. Keeping the Colt in his hand, he halted at the door, stepped to one side, and then kicked it open.

The door flew in, almost tearing from its rusted hinges. Inside the room, the girls were huddled together, half behind Mama Lupe, who stood glaring at the doorway like a malevolent mother hen. Fargo stepped inside in a quick motion. "Nobody moves," he growled.

Mama Lupe's eyes, hard as black rock, held on him. "You came in with that lieutenant," she slid out. "I remember you, *el hombre grande*."

Fargo moved toward the pile of army pistols on the floor. "Tomás and the other two?" she asked.

"*Muertos*," Fargo said. He dropped to one knee and began to take the cartridges from each of the army-issue Colts, push them into his shirt pocket. Mama Lupe continued to glare at him.

"It was their idea, stealing from the soldier boys," she said.

"Shit it was," Fargo snapped, emptying the last of the guns. He holstered his own Colt, met the cold hate in the woman's eyes. "Now you can all start carrying everything back to the wagon," he said.

The girls looked at the big woman. She jerked her head and shoulders in a giant shrug and her big body shook as though it were a giant pudding. "Do what he tells you," she said.

"You, too, Fatso," Fargo barked. "You're all in it together."

The girls moved, began to gather up uniform jackets and trousers from their separate piles. A tall girl started to pick up boots, putting one under each arm. Fargo saw Mama Lupe turn away from him, her broad back stained with perspiration. Another of the girls knelt down to gather up the small mound of watches and rings. Out of the corner of his eye, as he watched the girl, he saw Mama Lupe begin to turn back to him. He felt himself swear silently as he saw her hand coming out from between the fold of her voluminous breasts, a small-bore pistol clutched in it. He leaped sideways, using the powerful leg muscles and the lightning-quick reflexes that were his as the woman leveled the gun. The first shot slammed into the wall inches from his head and he twisted in the other direction as the girls screamed, dived away. The second shot splintered the wall by his head as he drew the Colt, dropped to one knee, and fired two shots. Mama Lupe's big body jerked as though a sudden spasm had seized her. One of the girls screamed as one of Mama Lupe's oversize breasts began to gush red, and suddenly the woman looked as though she were an obscene fountain.

Fargo saw her lips move soundlessly as she tried to aim the pistol again. His finger tightened on the Colt, but he held back a third shot as the woman swayed. Her breast gushing red with greater force, she sank down where she stood, the pistol falling from her hand, became an almost shapeless mass on the floor. The huge body shuddered for a last time and was still.

Fargo straightened up, saw the girls staring at the woman. "Take off your dresses," he barked harshly.

One girl brought her eyes up to him. "We don't have any more guns," she said.

"I'll make sure of it," Fargo said. "Get the damn dresses off."

Sullenly they pulled the dresses off. They were naked from the waist-up underneath, all wearing half-slips. "Lift the slips, all the way," Fargo ordered.

A tall girl with long, hanging breasts sneered at him. "You want to see our bushes, big boy?" she asked. "You want to pick out one of us?"

"I want to make sure none of you have a throwing knife in a leg sheath underneath those slips," Fargo said. "Come on, up with them. You're a little late to start being modest."

They glared as they lifted the half-slips and Fargo's glance swept along their legs. "All right, start loading the wagon again," he growled, stepped to the doorway, and watched as they began to carry the troopers' things to the wagon. They finished in three trips and Fargo hitched the pinto to the rear of the wagon and swung up onto the seat. The tall girl frowned up at him, alarm in her face.

"You can't leave us out here," she said.

"Guess again," he returned.

"We didn't do anything," another protested.

"You're a bunch of lying, thieving whores. You'd probably kill if it got you anything," Fargo said.

"What are we supposed to do with Mama Lupe?" the tall girl asked.

"Bury her. Make a monument out of her. Whatever you like. She's all yours," Fargo said, and snapped the reins. The horses started forward at once.

"Goddamn you," he heard the tall whore scream.

"*Bobolicón!*" another shouted, and he felt the two rocks hit the side of the wagon as he drove away. He kept going, turned down the passageway, and followed the wagon tracks back in the other direction this time. The dawn was pushing up into the night sky as he reached the town and drew up before the whorehouse. Vander and Herbst appeared at the sound of the wagon and Fargo swung to the ground.

"I brought back all their things," he said blandly.

"Jesus, we thought you'd gone back to camp," Herbst said in surprise.

"Was there trouble?" Vander asked.

"Some," Fargo said. "You got your boys awake enough to move?"

"Just about. They're still pretty foggy," Vander said. "I don't think they can dress themselves yet and they certainly can't ride."

"Dump them into the wagon," Fargo said. "They can sleep off the rest of it in camp before we move on."

He let Herbst and Vander lead the still-naked troopers into the wagon, where they sprawled limply. Vander drove while he and Herbst led their horses back to the camp as the day began to assert itself. The others woke as the wagon rolled in and Boswell and Crane helped unload the troopers. Carlita came down from behind the rocks in a peasant skirt and blouse, brushing her jet hair. She came to where Fargo unsaddled the pinto, studied his face. "*Malo, eh?*" she said.

"They were stupid, all of them," he said. "Make coffee. I want to wash, have coffee, and then move on."

"You are tired, *amigo*," she said.

"We can't waste a whole day sleeping. I'll catch up on rest tonight," he told her. She went to make coffee and he washed with cold water from his canteen, dousing himself and rubbing himself briskly. As he dried himself off, he saw Fern talking to Vander. Carlita returned with a mug of steaming coffee and he sipped it as she climbed up to get her bedroll from behind the rocks. He sat down with the coffee as Vander came over.

"You really thinking of moving out?" The man frowned. "The men are in very poor shape and I'm frankly exhausted, too."

"They'll be able to ride. So will you. We pull out in half an hour," Fargo said.

Vander hesitated, decided not to argue. He turned away and Fargo continued sipping his coffee, finally finished it, and let Carlita help him rub the pinto's back with witch hazel before resaddling the horse. She went to get her mount as Fern passed beside him.

"You were indeed right, it seems," she said, looking disgustingly fresh and pretty.

"It seems," he grunted.

"And we owe you thanks for getting the troopers' things back," she said. "You can do the right thing, can't you?"

"Right hadn't a damn thing to do with it. Ten naked soldier boys without guns are no damn good to anybody," Fargo growled.

"I see," she said stiffly.

"It's called honesty, honey." He grinned. "You ought to try it sometime."

"What does that mean?" she bristled.

"Whatever you want it to mean," he answered amiably.

She started to whirl away, paused. "Fern, damn you, the name is Fern, not honey," she said.

"I'll try to remember," he said, and watched her go off angrily, small, tight rear bouncing deliciously. He felt the tiredness inside him as he pulled himself into the saddle.

Carlita rode up beside him as he started from the

campsite. The troopers, most riding with heads hanging down, slumped low in their saddles, followed at a slow walk. Vander managed to sit ramrod-straight, Fern beside him. Boswell followed with Herbst and Crane. Fargo stayed on the Texas side of the border, keeping in the shade of the rock hills as much as possible, but by noon, when he halted at a water hole, Carlita's full, deep breasts were outlined by her perspiration-soaked blouse. Fern had shed her sleeveless vest, he saw, and the tiny points of her breasts pushed into her shirt, saucy, a very different line to them than Carlita's rounded bosom.

He allowed only a half-hour rest, saw that the troopers were regaining their strength, color coming back into their faces. The recuperative powers of youth, he grunted to himself, returned to the pinto, called to Vander. "Hug the rocks. I'm going on ahead," he said. He rode off without waiting for an answer, headed out onto the dry flatland. He disappeared into the haze of the heat, his eyes scanning the hot, dry ground. He found the tracks in a circle that moved wider each time and he cut across it, moved south, finally came to a halt again. He dismounted, picked up a kernel of dried corn, found another, and near both of them the unshod marks of the Indian ponies. He turned back, headed for the distant line of rocky hills that marked the Mexican side of the border and found the slow-moving line of weary riders.

It was nearly sundown and exhaustion pulled hard at him. Vander had lost his ramrod saddle position and gained Fern's sympathetic glances, Fargo saw. He pointed to a narrow passage leading into the rocky hills. "We make camp up there someplace," he said.

Vander found the strength to protest. "Ridiculous. We've an entire flat plain in front of us to make camp. We don't need to go climbing into the hills," he said.

"You make camp on that nice, flat plain and you could have company for breakfast," Fargo said.

Fern echoed Vander's frown and he saw Boswell move closer. "What kind of company?" the man asked.

"Apache. Mescalero. I saw signs of both and I don't much want either for breakfast," Fargo said. "Move 'em up." He urged the pinto on up the passageway and Carlita rode up to him, her peasant blouse clinging to her in a way it was never intended to do. Her black eyes took in his glance and the fatigue in his handsome face.

"All you can do is look tonight, *amigo*," she said, laughing.

He managed a rueful grin. "I'm afraid you're too damn right," he said. "I'm feeling stretched out, wrung out, and hung out." Her hand reached out, the back of it touching his cheek. He came on a long, narrow area between two tall boulders and he slid from the saddle. It would do well enough and he unsaddled the pinto, gave the horse water and some of the extra oats he always carried. He was too tired to think about eating and most of the others felt the same as camp was made in almost utter silence. He put his bedroll at a spot at the far end of the narrow area, saw Carlita place hers a few yards away. Fern and two of the troopers made a small fire to heat some beans and Fargo undressed quickly, was almost asleep when he felt Carlita drop to her knees at the edge of his bedroll.

"Tomorrow night we make up for lost time," she murmured, her voice full of promise. She rose and he opened one eye, watched her go to her bedroll and lie down. It was a nice promise to sleep on, and he did just that.

6

Fargo woke with the morning, stretched the powerful muscles of his shoulders, arched his back like a giant cat stirring itself. He had slept the deep, sound sleep of the exhausted and the body had renewed itself. He squinted down the narrow space. Carlita's bedroll was empty and two of the troopers were up making coffee, the others stirring. He caught a glimpse of red-blond hair lift itself from a blanket at the far edge of the space, and he rose, washed, walked over to the two troopers. "You see Señorita Orez?" he asked.

"No, sir," they said almost in unison. "Coffee?"

He took the mug, sipped from it as the others came to life. Vander appeared. He seemed to wake up looking pressed and polished, Fargo noted. Boswell came over with a nod and Fargo returned it. "Isn't it time you picked up some sign of Vilas?" the man asked.

Fargo shrugged. "Could be," he allowed, sauntered away as the others began to gather for coffee. Carlita hadn't returned to gather up her bedroll yet and he walked down to the end of the narrow space, climbed up over a rock. He halted as Fern stood in front of him, her skirt on, bare-shouldered in the top part of her slip. Broad shoulders, yet rounded and very feminine, he noted. She was vigorously brushing her hair and it shimmered in the morning sun. She became aware of some-one watching her, turned, a moment of alarm in her face, then her eyes narrowing at him.

"Obviously you don't believe in good manners," she said.

"I believe in enjoying myself," he said.

"Yes, so you've told me," she said sniffing.

"I see something beautiful to watch, I watch it, whether it's a sunset, a cluster of rose mallows, a scarlet tanager taking wing, or a good-looking woman," he remarked.

Her eyes turned a soft blue and she tossed him a slightly pleased look. "My heavens, do I detect a compliment?" she said.

He shrugged. "Just being honest." He smiled. He turned and left as she reached for her blouse, went back to the others. Carlita's bedroll had still not been touched and he walked over to it, felt the tiny frown start to touch his brow. Her black skirt lay beside the blanket and his glance moved to the ground just beyond the bottom edge of the bedroll. He knelt down as the frown dug deeper into his brow, his lips forming a soundless curse as he read the marks on the ground the way other men read a book. He swore again under his breath and the image leaped up in front of him, the lone night figure watching and following Carlita in Condor. He hadn't forgotten, he just hadn't found the right time to question her about it and now time had caught up to him. His eyes returned to the marks at the edge of the bedroll, narrowed, studying what they said in silence. One man, he muttered under his breath. Only one. He followed the footprints to where they led up to a path into the rocks above. It still stayed only one pair of boots and Carlita's sandaled tracks. He had walked close behind her, probably with a knife or gun held at her throat from behind.

Fargo heard Vander's voice call to him. "We're all set to move," the lieutenant said.

Fargo turned, took a stride toward the others. Fern, beside Vander, was about to climb on the gray mare. Boswell was already in the saddle and the troopers were lined up for Vander's signal to mount.

"Ready?" Vander asked.

"No," Fargo bit out, and saw the man's instant frown. "Carlita's gone. I'm going after her," Fargo said.

"What?" Vander asked incredulously.

"You have a hearing problem?" Fargo snapped. "Carlita's gone and I'm going after her. You can wait till I get back."

Fern's voice cut in, bitchiness wrapped around each word. "That explains this morning, your compliment and your excursion into pleasantness," she said. "I might have known."

"All you know is how to be wrong, Fern, honey," Fargo said.

Acid formed on her tone. "Your girlfriend ran off, so you decided a compliment might be in order. It's almost amusing. What happened? Didn't you pay up?" she flung at him.

"I'll remember that one later," Fargo promised, his voice cold steel. "Somebody took her."

Vander found his voice. "Somebody came into camp during the night and spirited her off?" He frowned. "You really expect us to believe that?"

Fargo's stare was hard rock. "I don't give a damn what you believe, but that's exactly what happened. A herd of buffalo could've come through and you wouldn't have woke, and I slept harder than I usually do. But he was good and now I'm going after her."

"Absolutely not," Fern snapped. "So she ran off with somebody. That's not our concern."

"I didn't say that. I said somebody took her out of here," Fargo returned.

Fern's face held imperiousness and bitchy smugness all at once. "Whatever, it's no matter to us," she said. "We're paying you to find Vilas and the saddle, not waste time chasing after one of your girlfriends."

Fargo met her stare with ice and swung up onto the pinto.

"You can't do this," he heard Fern half-shout, losing some of the imperiousness in her tone.

"Fern—Miss Blake, that is—she's right about this," Vander said stiffly. "This isn't part of our agreement and why we're paying you."

"Neither was my putting your soldier boys back together again," Fargo said, his voice growing into cold iron. "You don't like it? Fire me."

He waited, swept eyes of blue quartz across the group, saw the exchange of nervous glances. He uttered a short, harsh laugh, wheeled the pinto around, and started to ride away.

"What are we supposed to do, just sit here till you get back?" Vander called after him, petulance as much as frustration in his voice.

"Start a quilting bee," Fargo called back as he galloped from the camp scene. His eyes followed the marks on the dry dust ground. The kidnapper had been in too much of a hurry to get away. He'd left a trail clear as the new morning. One horse, Fargo noted. He was riding Carlita in the saddle with him. Bastard, Fargo swore to himself. The man had been good. He believed in giving every devil his due. Exhausted as he was, he would have heard most intruders. The bastard had to be experienced at stealth. Fargo's eyes saw the trail sweep up into the rock hills and he followed, keeping a steady pace. The man had at least three hours' head start, but it wasn't long before Fargo noticed the hoofprints growing closer together, the horse shortening stride rapidly. He followed on, interpreting the signs written in the dry dust ground. The man was making no effort to spur the horse on, he saw. He obviously realized the horse was struggling under two riders, and Fargo grunted in grim satisfaction.

By midday the man had stopped twice to rest the horse and Fargo knew his steady pace was closing in fast. The pinto, both fast and rugged, could handle the rock-hill riding. The trail led down suddenly, out of the hills, and Fargo espied the long stretch of condalias rising out of the bristle grass. He swung down onto the relative softness of the bristle grass, reined up after a half-hour to study a patch of pressed down grass. The rider had dismounted and the Trailsman's eye caught a set of new imprints leading from the spot, footprints pressing the grass down, one of boots, the other of sandals. Both Carlita and her kidnapper had taken to walking, the man leading the horse behind him. Fargo paused, knelt down to press his hand against the imprints in the grass. They were nearby, just ahead, the grassy imprints still half-dry.

Fargo stayed on foot, left the pinto, and glided forward in his long, loping stride, moving through the low condalia to suddenly hear Carlita's voice just ahead. "No, Santos, you *carcamán*," the girl half-screamed. "No, you leave me alone."

Fargo quickened his stride as Carlita cried out in pain this time and he heard the sound of a sharp slap. The two figures came into view and Fargo dropped to one knee beside one of the spiny-leafed low tree growths. Carlita lay on the ground, in her blouse and a half-slip, the man holding her down, half over her. With his leg, he rubbed upward and lifted the half-slip to bare one beautifully lithe, bronze-olive leg.

"*Mono peludo*, he is coming for me," Carlita spit at the man. "You touch me and he'll kill you."

The man drew his hand back, slapped her across the face. "Don't you try to lie to me. Nobody's coming for you," he snarled.

Carlita gasped, shook off the slap. "Fargo will come. I know he will," she insisted. "He'll know I didn't just go off alone."

The man half-rose, started to undo his pants. "Shut up. I've waited long enough for you. Now I'm going to enjoy myself," he said.

Carlita tried struggling, shifting to bring her leg around, but he pressed his thigh over her. "He'll come, damn you, Santos. He'll kill you," she gasped.

Fargo drew the Colt from its holster. "You better listen to the *señorita*," he called out quietly.

Carlita's head snapped around at once, her black eyes growing wide with joy. The man froze in place, not moving from atop her, slowly turning his head to look at where Fargo's bulk was barely visible behind the spiny leaves.

"Back off, mister," Fargo said.

Santos waited another moment, then slowly pulled his leg back. His left arm, on the other side of his body, was beyond Fargo's vision, but the Trailsman saw him start to push up from Carlita's form and suddenly he dropped forward down onto the girl again. Fargo caught the glint of the knife in his left hand as he pressed it across Carlita's throat as he lay on top of her.

"Throw out your gun or she's a dead one," the man ordered, pressed the knife down against Carlita's throat, and Fargo heard the girl's strangled cry of terror. "I'll cut her head off," Santos said, his voice rising.

No empty threat, Fargo realized. He had the Colt aimed directly on target, at the man's temple, but he held back squeezing the trigger as he swore to himself. The shot would set off a muscular reaction even as it killed him, one that would send the knife cutting through Carlita's throat. "The gun, *rápido*," Santos called out. "Throw it over here."

Fargo lowered the Colt. The man could only see his outlines through the condalia leaves. He emptied the shells from the gun, spun the chamber shut, and threw it out. It landed less than a foot away from the man. Santos pushed himself up from Carlita and scooped up the gun. "Now you come out, *papanatas*," he ordered.

Fargo rose, walked into the clear as Carlita scrambled to her feet, her eyes wide with fear again. Santos was taller than he'd thought, but spindly, a rapacious, thin face on him, Fargo noted as he moved toward the man.

"Put your hands in the air," the man ordered.

Fargo lifted his hands as he continued moving toward the man.

"That's far enough," Santos said, his forehead lowering as Fargo continued toward him. "Stop, damn you," the man shouted, consternation on his face as the big man kept walking at him. He raised the Colt a fraction higher. "Stop, you damnfool," he shouted, his face wreathed in a frown as Fargo continued walking toward him.

Santos fired, once, twice, his jaw dropping open as the hammer clicked against the empty chambers. He stared down at the gun in astonishment. His jaw was still hanging open when Fargo's blow smashed into it. The blow drove his jaw up into the top of his mouth and blood squirted from between his lips as he flew backward to hit the ground with shuddering impact.

Fargo reached him in one long stride, just as he started to get up. A looping left smashed his head sideways and Santos seemed to catapult through the air to land facedown. Fargo stepped toward him again, paused beside him, reached down, started to turn the man over when he twisted, let out a curse, stumbled away as the knife arc just grazed his wrist.

Santos drove himself forward, half-stumbling, his face a smear of swollen, misshapen red meat. He dived forward, the knife held like a short lance, and Fargo, twisted to the left, felt the blade rush past him. He brought his shoulder up and stuck out one leg. Santos toppled off-balance, hit the outstretched leg, and half-somersaulted forward.

The man's cry was a guttural scream, ending in a half-dozen gasped oaths. "Aaaaagh . . . agh . . . oh, god-damn, goddamn," Fargo heard him say, watched the fig-ure manage to turn his body. Both his hands were tightened around the hilt of the knife where it protruded from his belly. The figure quivered, legs drawing up, and slowly, reluctantly, the hands fell away from the knife. Fargo turned away, walked to where Carlita, only half-looking, her face averted, stood with arms wrapped close to herself. He said nothing, took her hand, and pulled her along with him until they reached the pinto.

"Get on," he said, and she climbed onto the saddle. He swung on behind her, trotted the horse until he was al-most at the end of the grass. He halted, took her down, and she looked up at the anger in the lake-blue eyes. "All right, I want the truth now. Who was he? Why did he come to take you back? You knew him in Condor. He was watching you there."

Her eyes widened in surprise. "You saw that?"

"I saw," he said. "Now talk."

Carlita's black eyes grew soft as twin, dark wells. "I'm sorry I did not tell you about Santos," she said. "I did not think it was important. I didn't think he'd follow me." Her hand came up to rest on Fargo's chest and he brushed it away, his eyes still cold.

"Go on," he muttered.

"Santos has been crazy for me for years. When Vilas

left me, he thought I would become his woman. I told him no, never, but he wouldn't believe that. He was always a little *majareta*, what you call crazy in the head. But I did not think he was this crazy." Her hands came up again to slide around Fargo's neck. "I knew you'd know I didn't just run off. And you came for me. You are a man of your word, Fargo, and I keep my promises." Her mouth reached up, opened for his lips, and he bent down, kissed her. "It is time for keeping promises," she murmured.

Fargo thought of the others waiting. They could wait a little longer, he murmured silently. Never put off till tomorrow what you can do today, he told himself. Some of those old proverbs made a lot of sense. He lifted her up with a sweep of his arms, put her down on the cool grass. She made a motion with one hand, pulling at strings, and the peasant blouse came undone and she flung it over her head. He let his eyes appreciate the beauty of the bronze-olive breasts, full and deep with rounded tops and bellied curves underneath, brown-pink nipples already standing high, large, light-brown circles around each one, a woman's breasts still full of the firm loveliness of girlhood.

Carlita's black eyes watched his enjoyment and he saw pride in her face, pride and the sensualist's desire to be wanted. Her hands reached down to the waist of the half-slip, pushed, and he watched the garment move down over a slightly curved, sensually fleshy little belly, then rise and fly into the air as she kicked it off with a quick motion of her legs. The black nap was thick, an overflowing triangle, an unruly garden of delight, completely appropriate to the overflowing sensuality that rose in waves from her gorgeous body. Her long, firmly fleshed legs lifted, opened, and quickly closed, and he caught the tiny sound of a low laugh that escaped her lips. He leaned over, pressed his mouth on hers, and she was wet and warm, her lips opening at once, drawing him in, a surrogate entrance, an appetizer for the senses. His tongue found hers, caressed around her, matching her little quivering motions. "Oh, *sí*, *sí*, Fargo . . . oh, *Dios mío*," she breathed.

He let his hands shed clothes and in moments he lay naked half-atop her, and she squirmed away, gazed at the beauty of his hard-muscled body, the powerful thighs, the tremendous rising of him; and she gasped, almost tore from his arms to fall across his groin, her lips finding him with gluttonous eagerness. "Oh, oh, ooooh, *sí*, oh, Jesús, Jesús," she murmured, and her shoulders rose and fell as she pulled on him with almost wild fervency until he reached down, yanked her away before he lost control.

She fell back breathing hard. "*Magnifico*, oh, so *magnifico*," she murmured and he closed his mouth around her left breast, drew the fullness of it in and his tongue traced a circle around the edges of the brown-pink areola. Her nipple was soft, much softer than he'd expected, and the bronze-olive skin was smooth as a ripe papaya. Her hands clutched at the back of his neck, then moved down along his shoulder blades, urging, smoothing and he heard her cries of pleasure as he sucked upon each breast. His hand moved down across the fleshy little mound of her belly, no fat, just the shape of her, all curves everywhere, all smooth sensuous shaping and he pressed down into the thick, black, luxurious nap. Her smooth, bronzed legs lifted, fell open. "Fargo, Fargo, quick, please, quick," she gasped out. He swung over her, plunged into her at once and was enveloped in wetness. Her hips lifted and she pumped her torso upwards, fell back and then her hips began to undulate, her legs rubbing in unison against him and he felt the circling contractions of her enveloping him in a delicious sensation.

Her eyes were open, bottomless black depths, and her full lips parted. "Ah . . . aaahh . . . aaaah . . . aaaah . . ." she breathed in rhythm with every undulating motion. He pushed forward as she revolved around him and he heard her cries begin to rise in pitch and then, with surprising force, her thighs clamped around his waist and her arms pulled him down to her. The undulating change to a fervent quivering as he closed his mouth around her breast and then the quivering exploded, in a paroxysm of pleasure. She cried out, a long, low cry, full of its own sensuality, that hung in the air, renewed itself with another paroxysm, and became almost a crooning gasp. No abrupt ending for her, he realized as her gasps stayed and the paroxysm came to a halt, but the little quiverings remained, only gradually lessening until finally she fell back and the black eyes stared up at him. A tiny smile came to touch her lips.

"*Maravilloso*," she murmured. "*Maravilloso*."

"You keep a pretty good promise yourself," Fargo said. He took in the dark-fire beauty of her as she lay nude beside him, all girl, all woman, a sensual admixture of the best of both. In five years she'd take on the heaviness that was part of her heritage, but now she was perfection. He lay back, her arm over his abdomen, soothing hands stroking gently. He saw the sun starting to slide across the afternoon sky. "We'd better start back," he told her, lifted himself up, and reached out for clothes. She pouted and he kissed her outthrust lips. "The night's not far away," he reminded. The pout vanished and she pulled the half-slip on, then the blouse, looked surprisingly demure in seconds.

They rode back along the bottom of the hills, cutting the time in half, and he saw the others get to their feet as he rode into camp. Carlita slipped from the pinto, started to gather her bedroll up and get her horse. Fern faced the Trailsman with hands on her hips, eyes as glinting as the red-blond hair. "I'm not even going to ask you what happened," she snapped.

"Good, because I don't aim to tell you," he said, and her lips bit into each other.

"Can we make the best of what's left of the day?" she asked sarcastically.

"I'm here waiting," he said mildly. She made a hissing sound and stalked to the gray mare to ride off beside Vander. Carlita, in a fresh blouse and her black skirt, rode up to Fargo, stayed with him as he cantered past Fern to take the lead. He glanced back, saw Herbst and Crane with Boswell moving up near Vander. He set a fast pace, but his eyes moved back and forth over the ground as he kept the line of riders at the edge of the hills. He pointed out a line of unshod pony tracks to Carlita and she nodded. The tracks were headed in the right direction, out across the flatland, and he kept on straight. It was nearing dusk when he drew to a halt as he picked up another cluster of tracks in the dry dirt, very faint, probably a week old. Carlita halted beside him as he dismounted.

"Five horses. Two packhorses," Fargo said.

"How do you know?" Vander asked as he rode up, Fern beside him.

"Two are heavily loaded, deeper hoofprints," Fargo said, running his fingers along the marks.

"Vilas," Vander said excitedly.

"No," Fargo said, glanced up at Carlita, saw the agreement in her eyes.

"It has to be," Vander said.

Fargo watched annoyance cross Carlita's face, chuckled to himself. "No," he said again.

"We know he had two packhorses with him. That makes five horses," Vander insisted.

"I can count," Fargo snapped.

"It does fit the reports," Herbst offered.

"Screw the reports. It's not Vilas," Fargo said, getting to his feet.

"Dammit, how can you be so sure," Crane cut in.

"Sure? I never use the word," Fargo said. "But these tracks go on out into the flatland. That wouldn't be Vilas. But it would be three silver prospectors and their packhorses coming out of the mountains."

He wheeled the pinto, his glance passing over Fern. Her face wore grudging acceptance along with a frown. He rode on, Carlita beside him, cast a glance at the girl. "He will stay in the mountains for a good while yet," she remarked. Fargo nodded, accepted the answer, and led the way to a gulley split up into three small areas by dividing rocks. Night was sweeping down quickly and he called a halt.

"This'll have to do," he said, Vander took his troopers to the first of the areas and saw to unsaddling the mounts. Boswell, Crane, and Herbst tethered their horses in the middle section, and Fern rode past the dividing rock formation to the last, smallest area. Carlita followed and Fargo entered after her. Fern had her bedroll laid out while he was still unsaddling the pinto.

"I suggest cold rations tonight and an early start in the morning," she said, her tone an order.

"Suits me," Fargo agreed. He saw Carlita spread her bedroll atop a little edge a few feet up as darkness descended on the campsite. He moved up to join Carlita as the night air quickly became cool. Undressing, he slid under the light blanket to find Carlita already naked. She pressed against him at once, her lips finding his mouth, pulling, sucking, demanding his tongue. Her hand reached down between his legs and she uttered a tiny gasp as she found him responding instantly. Her firm-thighed legs fell open and her little convex belly rose up as the feverish urgency flowed from her.

He turned, came into her immediately, and she cried

out in pleasure as she moved with him. He pulled back and forth inside her, quick, sharp motions to match her eager hurrying. The cries of pure delight began to come from her, each a little stronger. "Aiiieee . . . aaaiiieee . . . aiieeee . . . oh, Jesús . . . oh . . . aiiieee." Each match a ramrod thrust and her hips lifted, pushed forward, matching him with reckless ecstasy.

He slowed as he heard the sound from below, a muttered oath, flicked a glance down to see Fern, blanket wrapped around her, striding away to disappear behind the other side of the dividing rock. He half-grinned, resumed the rhythmic pleasures, and once again Carlita's gasped cries echoed out. Suddenly he felt her pause, the quivering begin, and she pressed hard against him as he increased tempo, finding the moment just as she screamed in pleasure and pulled his mouth down to her breasts. "Aaaaaiiiieeeeee . . . oh, Fargo, oh Dios," she breathed, and once again the little quiverings stayed with her until slowly they became less.

Finally he moved beside her. She was asleep in moments, one leg over him, the deep, full breasts soft against his chest. The cool night wind became a lullaby and the little gulley grew silent.

7

He slept well, to wake with the dawn. Carlita still lay hard asleep and he took a moment to lift the blanket and enjoy the beauty of her, then slipped from the bedroll and pulled on trousers. A patch-nosed snake wandered across the ground and Fargo sat up, saw that its yellow and brown stripes were glistening with a film of water. He stood up just as Fern came around from the other side of the divider rock, the blanket still wrapped around her, red-blond hair a flash of brilliance in the early sun. He saw her watch him move up along the rocks, following the snake's winding trail. He disappeared from her sight, saw the trail half-circle around a cluster of sharp-edged stones, and followed. He halted at the other side of the stones, smiled quietly at the oblong pool of water that appeared as if by magic. The magic was an underground spring, and he kicked off trousers and sank into the water, still chilled from the night. The pool was deep and he treaded water, sank below the surface, came up, let the travel dust wash from him, sank below again. This time when he came up he saw Fern there, watching barefoot, but she'd slipped on trousers and a green blouse.

He tossed her a wide grin. "Come on in," he said, moving toward the edge of the mountain spring pool.

"I'll wait my turn, thank you," she said severely, and he saw the anger in her eyes that watched him.

"What made you move last night? That spot too hard?" he asked innocently, and the blue eyes flashed. "Or did something else bother you?"

"I wasn't *bothered* by anything, not the way you mean," she said haughtily.

"Sure about that?" He grinned.

"Quite sure. I just like quiet when I sleep," she said.

"Sorry about that. I can't help being good," he remarked.

"If that was the case," she said, and he frowned in question. "Perhaps your girlfriend's just noisy," she tossed out.

"One for you." Fargo grinned back, stepped out of the water. He saw her eyes go down to the way his wet trunks clung to his groin, outlining every part of his equipment, and she spun around, hurried away as he chuckled. He scooped up his trousers and started back down the rocks to the campsite, reached Carlita, who had wakened, eyed him appreciatively as she handed him a towel. He dried himself, dressed, and saw the others had come awake. Vander came around the dividing rocks to approach him.

"Fern tells me there's a mountain spring pool," he said. "We'll all appreciate that. Ladies, first, of course," he said, turning to Carlita.

She flashed a smile that would melt a rock. "*Gracias,*" she said. She took the towel back and started up toward the pool as Fargo took the time to rub down the pinto. The troopers were last to make use of the pool and they were quick at it.

Fargo led the group out of the gulley before the sun began to rise high in the morning sky. Fargo headed along a narrow trail that wandered through the lower reaches of the rock hills and Vander, with Herbst and Crane, cantered up to him.

"Vilas was in a hurry," Vander said. "He'd stay along the flatland."

"This is a damn slow trail," Herbst put in.

Fargo looked at Carlita. "He would take this way," she said.

"Dammit, Fargo, you're supposed to be finding him for us," Vander exploded. "Instead, you're going along with whatever this girl says."

"She knows him. She's told me about him. I agree with her. Vilas would put caution ahead of speed," Fargo said. He spurred the pinto on without waiting for further discussion and Carlita went with him. The others grumbled but fell into line behind, and he snaked his way through the narrow passage, halting at a small clearing where half-burned branches formed the remains of a fire. He gestured to marks to one side as Vander rode up with Fern, Herbst, and Crane just behind him.

"Five horses waited over there, two packhorses," he said.

"At last we're on his trail," Vander said.

"It looks like it," Fargo commented, moving forward again. He caught Fern's frown as she watched and a few minutes later she rode up to him, ignoring Carlita.

"What did that mean back there?" she asked waspishly. "What does 'It looks like it' mean?"

"It means signs are signs. You read them and hope you're right until you get something more to hang on to," he told her affably. She studied him for another minute, her soft blue eyes probing, trying to see past his words, and finally she turned the gray mare and rode back to Vander and the others.

Fargo heard Carlita's soft laugh. "She does not trust you, *amigo*," the girl said. "But she wouldn't trust any man she could not hold in her hand."

"Probably," Fargo agreed, and smiled inside himself. Fern didn't trust him, but she was working out of a wellspring of acute intuition. Carlita hadn't picked up the ambiguousness in his remark and he cast a glance at her. "How come you didn't ask about that?" he questioned casually.

The girl shrugged. "I understood," she said, and again Fargo smiled inside himself. How many other things had she just neglected to mention, such as her suitor, Santos, he pondered, quietly amused. Carlita wanted to get to Vilas as desperately as the others and she wouldn't be above playing her own games to do so. He'd bought her story, brought her along, paid attention to her suggestions, but he trusted her only a little more than the others, a fact she failed to realize. Her explanation for Santos, her crazed suitor, had been a masterpiece of quick thinking, full of reasonable explanation. But the explanation was all on the surface. There were holes underneath. Carlita was a creature of back streets and dusty grubby little towns. Perhaps a little dishonesty was just part of her makeup. In a bedroll there was no deceit to her and he was still glad he'd brought her. She had more than delivered on that promise.

He rode till the day began to edge toward dusk. The terrain was hard riding and he saw the effects on Vander's young troopers, their faces drawn tight. The character of the rock hills had shifted. Oblong mesas became more frequent with cholla and yucca more plentiful, and the rocks themselves had grown into boulders and sides of stone. More small passages wove in and out as the hills became rock mountains.

He struck camp for the night on a small mesa with enough brush for firewood. Fern put her bedroll on the other side of the site from where Carlita had spread hers and glared at the grin Fargo tossed her. After the others had fallen asleep, he pulled Carlita's things up into one of the small passageways and lay down beside her. Once again, the devouring hunger in her leaped into action and she turned the dark into fire, pleasure into a wild and consuming ecstasy. Only as the moon rose high in the sky did he lay beside her, his head across her soft-pillow breasts, and joined her in the deep, satisfied breathing of sleep.

The morning sun came too soon and he woke, dressed, saw Vander dressed, his troopers pulling themselves into shape to ride. Fargo had a mug of coffee one of the troopers offered, studied the young face. Vander came up, sipping his coffee. "Why'd the army send you a pack of boys out here?" Fargo asked the lieutenant.

"The experienced troopers are being kept back north of the Mississippi, except for those in Indian territory," the man replied.

"Why?" Fargo questioned.

"There's talk of war between the states. Surely you've heard some of it," Vander said.

"A little," Fargo allowed. "But I don't pay much mind to rumors."

"I guess the army thinks there's more than rumour to it," Vander said. "They're sending all new recruits out in the field to replace experienced men they're drawing back."

Fargo nodded, frowned in thought for a moment. A war between the states would be a bitter business and leave much of the territory lands to shift for themselves. Some of the most warlike tribes would take advantage of that. So would a lot of other people, Fargo pondered.

Vander's voice cut into his thoughts. "You haven't said you've come onto any further signs of Vilas," the man commented.

"There were a few," Fargo told him, tracks of the same five horses he had seen twice during yesterday's riding. He finished the coffee as Fern appeared and

75

looked bright and pretty as a new penny. "Sleep well last night?" he asked.

"Very well," she said almost disdainfully. Vander took her arm and led her to where the trooper held the coffeepot.

Fargo saddled the pinto and Carlita appeared and tossed him a quick smile made of echoes of the night. She mounted her horse as Fargo swung onto the pinto. His eyes swept the rock of the mountains, one pathway leading along the side of the mesa, another climbing up higher.

Carlita read his thoughts. "The one going higher," she said.

He let his glance hang on Carlita as Fern and Vander rode up. She looked back at him with quiet confidence. "Why?" he asked. "He'd make better time on the low road."

"*Sí*," she agreed. "That is what anyone following would think and so he would not take it. Never do what they expect you to do, he tell me once."

Fargo turned her words over in his mind. Vilas could well be capable of that kind of cleverness. Those always on the run develop their own brand of protective thinking. "All right, you start up the high road," he said to Vander. "I'll catch up to you." He turned the pinto to move along the mesa road, saw Carlita start to follow. "No, you ride with the others," he said, and saw the surprise in her eyes, almost hurt in the black pool depths. His face remained unyielding and she gave a little shrug, turned, and went with the others as they started upward.

Fargo cantered on along the lower, straighter road, his eyes sweeping the ground as he rode. He'd gone perhaps a half-hour when he reined to a halt. Along the side of the road, where two rocks formed a hollow, the remains of a campfire nestled. He dismounted, examined the ground nearby. Three horses, he muttered to himself. A tiny, hard-edge smile touched his mouth. He rose, scanned the rocky mountain area, eyes narrowed; and he remounted, rode back the way he'd come, and took the high road. He caught up to the line of troopers, rode past them, came abreast of Boswell and Herbst.

"Satisfied we're on the right road?" Boswell asked.

"Satisfied enough," he said, and rode on to pause before Carlita. She nodded to him, followed after him as he rode out ahead of the others. The boulders took on a rounder contour and he rode along a wide, arroyolike path. He halted in the early-afternoon sun to rest the horses where a cluster of manzanita bushes offered some shade. His eyes swept the top of the rocks and a frown touched his forehead. Two whip-tailed lizards scurried down from the top of the rocks. He'd seen two more a little while back, and as he watched, a horned lizard slowly moved from the rocks to climb downward, resembling a miniature prehistoric monster. Fargo remounted, led the way forward again, and his eyes continued to scan the rocks. Two ground utas scurried down, one showing the pale-blue underside of a male as he hopped from one rock to another. A little farther on, Fargo glimpsed the green of a spiny iguana moving slowly down from the upper ledge of rock.

Fargo's eyes took on a blue-quartz hardness and he dropped back to where Vander rode in casual conversation with Fern. "We've got company," Fargo muttered.

"Vilas?" the lieutenant said, excited instantly.

"Hell, no, but company," Fargo said. "Up along the top of the rocks there."

Vander's eyes swept the rounded boulders. "I don't see a thing." He frowned.

"I do," Fargo bit out.

"What do you see?" Fern questioned.

Fargo nodded to a four-foot coachwhip snake that

came into view, slithered down from the rocks, its yellow stripes gleaming in the sun.

"That?" she frowned.

"That's one more. There's been a small parade of mountain wildlife suddenly moving down from the rocks. They don't all suddenly move like that. Something's disturbing them up there, like horses and humans," Fargo said.

"I'll put my men at the ready at once," Vander said, started to turn in the saddle.

"No, dammit," Fargo hissed. "That's just why I came back here. You keep your boys nice and quiet. No gunplay, no heroics."

The lieutenant stared, wrestling with the official military procedures manual that was engraved inside him.

"I don't know what kind of company we've got, but they won't be gentlemen," Fargo said, and rose on to the front of the column beside Carlita. Her glance at him was sharp.

"What's the matter?" she asked. "You are bothered."

"I am," Fargo said, his tone cutting off further questions. He held the reins with his left hand, his right resting at the butt of the Colt. His eyes narrowed, held at the end of the arroyo, and he was waiting, expecting, as the four horsemen came into view, moving out from behind a slab of rock. The riders halted, blocking the path, and Fargo took in the man in the center. He saw a tall man, thick black hair, black eyes, and a straight nose, good-looking in a very Mexican way. He wore a shirt of tan trimmed with fringed tassels in the Mexican fashion. Only a hardness in his mouth marred the somewhat dashing picture he gave. The other three were mean-eyed vaqueros, one carrying a cartridge belt slung across his chest.

Fargo halted, felt the others come up behind him. "Bandidos," he murmured.

The man with the fringed shirt looked at Carlita, then at Fargo, his lips tightening. "I am Carlos Bracca," he said, his voice low, sonorous.

"Some people call him Bracca the Bandit," Carlita said. Fargo saw the man slowly smile at the title.

"So they do," he agreed.

Fargo's eyes snapped sideways as Carlita dug heels into her horse, sent the animal leaping forward. He felt the astonishment flood his face as she raced to the bandit's side, reined up, and leaned over, flung her arms around the man, and pressed her mouth on his in a fervent kiss. Fargo felt the frown still digging deeper into his brow as the man finally pushed her away.

"I underestimated you, my little Carlita," Carlos Bracca said, a slow smile touching his mouth again. Fargo watched him reach a hand out, pat her cheek. "All right, I admire such determination. Go back with Pedro and the others," the man said, and Fargo saw Carlita move her horse back to stand beside the vaquero with the extra cartridge belt.

"Goddamn," Fargo muttered, the answers not all in place but enough beginning to form to make him seethe with rage. Bracca's voice brought his thoughts back to the moment.

"These are my hills, *amigos*," the man said quietly.

"I didn't see your name anyplace," Fargo answered with matching quietness.

"You are seeing it now," Bracca said. "Who are you?"

"Fargo. Some people call me the Trailsman," Fargo said.

"You lead the others, including the *soldados*," Bracca said, curiosity in his voice.

"That's right," Fargo said, meeting the bandit leader's glittering black eyes with unfazed calm, pushing down the fury inside him that continued to rage at Carlita Orez.

"Well, then, Trailsman, this will be a very expensive trail for you, for all of you," Bracca said almost pleasantly.

Fargo's mind raced. The bandit had a lot more than three vaqueros with him, he knew, but he decided it was time to make him play at least a few of his cards. "Maybe not, my friend," Fargo remarked. "Or is Bracca so powerful he can ignore ten troopers and five more guns?"

The man's slow smile crossed his face again. "Bracca ignores nothing, especially what you call firepower," he said, and Fargo saw his eyes shift to Fern. "But right now, three guns are aimed at the lovely blond *señorita*," he said, raised his arm, and Fargo glanced up at the top of the rocks to see the line of horsemen appear, each with a rifle. He counted eight in a sweeping glance, the first three, as Bracca had said, with their rifles trained on Fern. Fargo saw her face go pale for an instant. He returned his eyes to Bracca.

The man half-shrugged apologetically. "A precaution," the bandit leader said. "Any sudden moves by you or the troopers would be most unfortunate for the *señorita*."

"Of course," Fargo said, wanting nothing more than he'd learned for the moment, that Bracca commanded a force of twelve cutthroats. "What's your price?" he asked.

"All your money, all your guns, all the troopers' rifles and horses," the man said.

"I can't decide that," Fargo told him. "That'll take talking about."

Bracca cast an eye at the gathering dusk. "It will be dark soon. You have till dawn tomorrow to decide," he said. "You'll camp here. Just to make sure you try nothing foolish, the blond *señorita* will come with us."

Fargo watched Fern's eyes grow wide in fright, go

from him to Vander and back to him. "You can't let him take me," she said. "Aren't you going to stand up to him at all?"

"Nope," Fargo said.

"Well, I certainly will," Vander said angrily, moving his horse forward to Fern. "You won't take her anywhere," he called to Bracca.

The bandit leader shrugged. "Then we start the fighting now and she will be the first one killed for sure," he said.

Vander's face flushed and his lips moved soundlessly. Fargo saw Fern's eyes on him again.

"Go with them," Fargo said quietly, reached out, gave the gray mare's reins a tug. The horse moved toward Bracca. "That's why I never bluff with an empty hand," Fargo told her as she passed. She let her eyes hold his for a moment, saw the hard glints deep in their blue depths, unsaid words, and she went on.

One of Bracca's vaqueros took the mare's bridle in hand and they started to move up behind the rocks. Fargo watched Carlita ride off with the bandit leader, not glancing back. Stinking little bitch, he murmured to himself, a rueful admiration in the words. He'd never been all that certain of her reasons for coming along, the story about Santos only one of the holes, but he hadn't expected this. She had played her hand well, too dammed well.

He watched as the line of vaqueros on the edge of the rocks moved back out of sight, turned to Vander and the others.

"What in hell can we do?" Boswell asked at once.

"Lay low, take the time he gave us to get ready. When morning comes, my troopers will rush them," Vander said.

Fargo saw Crane and Herbst looking at him. He dismounted, led the pinto to the side. "Let's make camp," he said.

"Are you saying you agree with Lieutenant Vander's plan?" Herbst asked as he dismounted.

"Shit, no," Fargo said quietly, saw Vander's face darken.

"I know my troopers. I've confidence in them whether you do or not," the lieutenant said.

Fargo fastened Vander with a contemptuous stare. "You think Bracca is going to let Fern just sit on the sidelines, come morning?" he asked. "He's going to have her at gunpoint just as he did now. She'd be dead before your boy-troopers got halfway up to him."

Vander lapsed in sullen silence and Fargo drew some hardtack from his saddlebag and cut off a piece.

"What are you thinking of doing?" Boswell said, sitting down beside him as the night cloaked the area and Vander saw to the troopers. Herbst and Crane came over to listen. "And what about that Carlita Orez?" Boswell asked. "You let her lead us right into this, Fargo." The Trailsman threw the man a hard glance but knew he was half-right. "What are you going to do?" Boswell pressed.

"I don't know. Sleep on it, maybe come up with an idea before morning," Fargo said. He saw Boswell and the two men exchange unhappy glances as they walked away. He sat back. They could think whatever the hell they pleased. He'd say nothing more. He wanted no arguments, no second-guesses, and most of all, no more surprises. Truth was in even shorter supply than he'd realized on this expedition, he grunted, thinking again of Carlita. He shifted position, lay down, took off his gun belt, and pushed his hat over his face. He seemed to sleep, and eyes closed, he waited silently, listened to the slow sound of the others finally sleeping. It took longer than usual, but the camp finally fell into stillness and

Fargo pushed the hat from his face. His eyes went skyward, saw the three-quarter moon moving westward. He pushed himself up to a sitting position, his glance scanning the camp. The troopers slept along one side, by their mounts, and he made out the figures of Boswell, Herbst, and Crane in their bedrolls nearby. Vander bedded down with his men.

Fargo rose, silent as a puma on the prowl. He adjusted his gun belt so there was no chance for it to rub against his trouser belt. He wrapped a few pieces of loose change he had in a kerchief, stuck it securely into his pocket. Crouched, he began to move along the edge of the area to the end where the path moved upward to the rocks above. Bracca had gone up that way and Fargo climbed upon a nearby rock, began to climb from rock to rock alongside the passageway. When he reached the top he was still in the rock crevices, but he could see the figure squatting at the top of the passageway, rifle held across its lap. There'd be another sentry at the far end by any passage there, he knew, but that was no concern now.

His eyes swept the flat rock table, saw most of Bracca's vaqueros asleep in a semicircle. He picked out Bracca, in a serape, asleep alone near the edge of the rocks. Three guards were standing around a blanketed figure on the ground, and even in the dim light he could see Fern's strawberry-blond hair, a dull red now. He swore under his breath. Three of them. Too many and all awake and watching over her. He swept the site again, frowning, found the figure half under a manzanita bush, sleeping without a blanket. And alone. Bracca had taken Carlita in but was still keeping her at a distance. Fargo returned his eyes to the first sentry at the top of the passageway. He stepped from between the rocks and dropped to his stomach, taking the Colt out as he did, to hold it by the barrel.

Slowly he began to crawl forward. Silence was everything. Even a garrote was too risky. A gagged half-cry, a garbled sound, and everything would go up in smoke. Silence, absolute silence. The three guards around Fern were far enough away not to be a factor yet and he crawled forward, an inch at a time, sliding his body along the flat rock, freezing every time the man shifted position. It seemed hours, but he knew it was only minutes when he neared the squatting figure. The man had been ordered to keep his eyes glued down the passageway and he was obeying orders. Fargo rose onto the balls of his feet, the guard less than a foot away from him now at the top of the passageway. He took one silent step forward and brought the butt of the Colt down on the man's skull. He half-dived, caught the rifle before it fell onto the rock, got his other hand onto the man's shirt, and eased the limp form to the ground.

He dragged the unconscious figure a few feet down the passageway and, the rifle in his hand, returned to the flat table of rock above. Once more he dropped to his stomach and began to crawl, this time to the lone manzanita bush and Carlita sleeping beside it. He halted for a moment, his eyes moving to Fern and the three guards surrounding her, and swore inwardly again. There was no way he could take her in silence. Bracca had made sure she'd stay in his hands. Fargo crept forward again, reached Carlita. She slept in her half-slip and her blouse unbuttoned, the beautiful bronzed-olive breasts in full view, and he remembered the night before with her. Damn lying little bitch, he swore to himself again. He pushed the rifle forward, pressed the end of the barrel against her forehead as he clapped a hand over her mouth.

Her eyes snapped open in fright and took a moment to focus on him. He saw the realization come into them as he kept the rifle barrel hard against her forehead. He whispered, his voice barely audible, but only an inch from his lips, she could hear him without trouble.

"You're coming with me," he said. "One sound and I'll blow your lovely head away." He let her read his eyes. "I don't want to, my little Carlita, but I'll do it. You once called me *peligroso*. You wouldn't want me for an enemy. You were right, there," he reminded her. "*Comprende?*" he asked, emphasizing the question with a push on the rifle barrel.

She nodded and he saw the fear in her eyes. Carlita Orez had the wisdom of the untutored in her. She knew he meant every word. He yanked her up, pressed the rifle against the back of her head. "Crawl, on your lovely little belly," he hissed, and she began to inch along the rock. He crawled with her, half on top of her, the rifle held against the back of her head until they reached the passageway. He rose to his feet, yanked her up, paused to glance at the unconscious figure. He smashed the rifle butt on the man's head again just for good measure and pushed Carlita down the passage ahead of him.

When he reached the bottom and emerged onto the arroyo, he saw one of the troopers move, rifle ready to fire. "It's me," he called softly, moved forward with Carlita. He saw Boswell come awake, then Vander and the others. They stared at Carlita. "I went and got her," he said.

"Her?" Vander frowned. "Why in God's name didn't you bring back Fern?"

"Because he's got a heavy guard around Fern. There wasn't a chance of pulling it off. But now maybe we can bargain with Bracca. Maybe," Fargo said.

"You've a plan," Herbst said.

"Yes, but first Carlita and I are going to have a private talk," he said, took the girl by her thick, jet hair, and pulled her along with him to the far end of the arroyo.

He flung her to the ground and he saw the fear in her eyes again, anger mixed in with it this time.

"Out with it, damn you," he rasped. "Start with Santos. He was no crazy lover. I knew that much all along."

Surprise came into her face. "How?" she asked.

"You know how to make up stories, but you don't know much about how people behave. A man crazy with desire for you, the way you painted Santos, would have gone after you in town, probably killed you when you turned him down. Santos was only keeping tabs on you. He was no love-crazed suitor and you never turned him down. Only after you managed to throw in with me did he have to come after you. He was Bracca's man, wasn't he?"

She glowered up at him. "Sí," she admitted. "Carlos wouldn't take me with him. We had a big fight over it. He knows me, so he left Santos to make sure I didn't try to follow after him."

"So you saw a chance by going with me," Fargo bit out. "You gave me that phony story about being rejected by Vilas and your need for revenge. I ought to wring your goddamn neck."

Protest leaped into her eyes. "The things I told you about Vilas were true," she said. "I know him, too. He has come this way. He and Carlos are friendly. He would have nothing to fear by taking the mountain path. He has come this way, I tell you. He is not very far ahead of you."

"I know that, too," Fargo said, and once again surprise flooded into her face. He reached down, yanked her to her feet. "You're one headstrong, stubborn little package," he said. "I can see why Bracca didn't want you along." He paused, his eyes narrowing in thought. He knew the truth about her relationship to Bracca now, and his mouth turned down in grim disappointment. She mightn't do him much good at all, he realized. But he'd have to make the best of it. Maybe Bracca had enough care for her. Maybe, he grunted pessimistically as he pulled her back to where Vander and the others were clustered.

"Come morning, we're going to try and bargain with Bracca," he said.

"Fern for her?" Boswell said. "Brilliant."

"Maybe a waste of time," Fargo said, Boswell frowning back. "It'll work only if he cares about what happens to her."

"He cares," Carlita snapped. "Carlos cares for me. He just doesn't want a woman when he goes into the mountains."

"He cares?" Fargo echoed. "We'll find out, come morning." He turned back to the others. "I'm not sure he gives a damn what happens to her. If I'm right, we've got nothing to bargain with. I'm going to keep on thinking I'm right, which means there's only one other chance left."

"What's that?" Vander asked.

"To get Fern when the fighting starts. I'll have to be ready, in position, and move fast. A lot of luck will help, too," Fargo said. "First, tie her up, hands and feet," he ordered, and Vander had two of his troopers do the job. "Come morning, it's going to be a matter of split-second timing," Fargo said. "You and your troopers do your job right and I'll have a chance."

"You can count on my men," Vander said with his usual pomposity.

Fargo winced inwardly but said nothing and began to detail his plan. He spoke tersely, holding out nothing but the barest chance of success. When he finished, Vander's face was least grim. Conceit was a great help sometimes, Fargo muttered to himself.

"I'll have everyone in position," Vander said.

"I'll hear you from where I am, come morning. You

just follow through," Fargo said. He started to turn, move toward the passageway at the end of the arroyo.

"Good luck," Herbst called after him, and Fargo nodded as he quickened his long, loping stride. He took the passageway this time, slowed only when he neared the top. The crumpled form of the sentry still lay against one side and Fargo crossed to the rocks, slipped into a crevice, found another, clambered up onto still another, and squinted across the flat area. The three guards were still around Fern, the others still asleep. Fargo leaned back into the crevice, sank down, and half-closed his eyes. He had few hours left till dawn and he took advantage of them, slept the way a mountain lion sleeps, the body at rest, the senses awake. Dawn would come soon enough.

8

Fargo's eyes came open as the first shaft of sun struck the rocks. He was on his feet in the crevice, the big Colt in hand, as the shout of alarm went up. He peered out from between the narrow crevice to see the sentry's form being pulled up from the passageway. Bracca, on his feet, his face flushed with dark anger, spun around to look toward Fern, first, then at Carlita's empty bedroll. He walked to the still unconscious form of the sentry and kicked it viciously. "*¡Estúpido! ¡Cretino!*" he snarled. He turned to the others who were gathering together, frowning in surprise as realization dawned on them. Fern sat up. She hadn't been tied, Fargo saw.

Bracca motioned to his vaqueros and they moved to the edge of the rocks with him, all but one, who stayed guarding Fern, rifle in hand. Bracca looked down to the arroyo below as Fargo watched, listened. If Vander had followed his orders, Bracca would see Carlita first, bound hand and foot and propped up against a rock. Then he'd see the troopers lined up against the side of the rocks, rifles pointed upward. Fargo brought the Colt up as he heard Bracca call down to Vander.

"Where is the big *hombre* . . . Fargo?" the man asked.

"Close enough," Fargo heard Vander answer.

"He was the one, I know it," the bandit leader said, and Vander remained silent. "My price is the same," Bracca said.

"But things are different now. We have the *señorita*, as you see," Vander called back.

Fargo saw Bracca half-laugh. "You think you have made what you call a standoff, eh?" the man said.

"I'd say so," Vander answered. "Harm Miss Blake and the *señorita* will pay the price."

Fargo edged close to the end of the crevice, saw Bracca's slow, cold smile. "That is too bad. I will be sorry to see that happen," the bandit said.

"Carlos!" Fargo heard Carlita cry out.

"It changes nothing," Bracca said, his voice growing hard. "The *señoritas* will both pay the price."

"*Sinvergüenza*," Fargo heard Carlita scream. "*¡Canalla!* Rotten, bloodsucking leech."

Bracca, ignoring her, barked down at Vander. "Your move, *soldado*," he said.

Fargo cursed silently. There'd be no bargaining. His guess had been all too accurate. Bracca didn't give a damn about using Carlita, tossing her away if he had to. The Trailsman's jaw muscles grew tight as he moved to the very edge of the crevice.

Carlita still screamed curses and Bracca waited confidently for Vander's answer. Fargo raised the Colt. Vander's next move had been marked out for him last night, the word whispered to his troopers behind him: "*Fire.*" Fargo took aim, waited for the explosion of sound. A second more passed and suddenly the air seemed to burst open as the volley of rifle fire from below resounded against the rocks.

Bracca dived, twisted away as two of his vaqueros fell. On the ground he snarled a shout at the guard beside Fern. "Shoot her now, shoot," he yelled.

The man raised his rifle and Fern, on one knee, stared

in horror at the barrel. Fargo's shot, already aimed, blew the back of the rifleman's head away and the man's hair flew off as though it were a red-and-black star burst. His body pitched forward as Fern twisted out of the way.

Fargo leaped from the crevice and she saw him. "Run. This way," he yelled.

As she started to race toward him, he dropped to one knee, laid down a barrage of covering fire that made Bracca, trying to get his own gun, roll for safety and two of his men dive away. Fern fell as she reached him, Fargo grabbed her arm, yanked her into the crevice with him as he fell backward. Four shots slammed into the rock inches from where he'd been as he reloaded the Colt. Fern lay half across his leg as he saw one of the bandits come into sight. He fired over her and the bandit doubled in two as the bullet ripped into his abdomen.

Vander was following orders, his troopers firing in continuous volleys, and Fargo, on his feet again, pulled Fern deeper into the crevice. She came against him, trembling, wet with the perspiration of fear, and her breasts pressed soft points into his chest. Bracca's vaqueros were returning fire, but their shots were sporadic and uncoordinated. Vander had the troopers firing blanket volleys at the top of the rocks, keeping up a steady hail of lead, and suddenly one of the bandits came into view, dropped to one knee, his rifle aimed into the crevice. Fargo fired two shots instantly as a second bandit came up behind the first. The rifleman's chest burst into a cascade of red as his torso twisted, slammed into the man behind him, who staggered back off balance.

Fargo heard Bracca's voice shouting commands, caught the word *caballo*. Staying low, he peered out past the edge of the crevice. Bracca was already in the saddle as the others leaped onto their horses. Fargo counted six lifeless bandits left behind as Bracca led the others galloping toward a passageway at the rear of the rock wall.

He aimed, fired, and made it seven as a vaquero with a red shirt spilled out of his saddle, to lay quivering on the ground, the red shirt becoming redder.

Fargo stepped from the crevice as the last rider disappeared up the passage behind the rock wall. The sound of the horses faded slowly in the echo chamber of the hills. He turned to look at Fern. She stood against the rock wall, eyes wide on him, letting the trembling come to a halt. Slowly she came to him, halted to peer into his eyes. He gave her no time to grope for words and started down the passageway.

"You coming?" he called brusquely, and she shook herself, moved to follow him. Her eyes were still wide, he saw, her face filled with soberness. She had looked into the face of death, saw life slipping away at the end of a rifle barrel. That kind of thing stayed hard inside one when one wasn't used to it, and he let her follow along without trying to hand any words of comfort. There was no need and no good that'd come of it. The shock would pass off in its own time. The others waited at the arroyo, rushed forward to greet them, Boswell wrapping his arms around Fern, hugging her to him.

"Thank God you're safe. We didn't know. We could only hope," he said, and she nodded silently.

"You were right about Bracca all along," he said, turning to Fargo, and the Trailsman caught Vander's still face.

"How many?" he asked.

"Two. Troopers Clark and Himan," the lieutenant said.

"Could've been worse," Fargo grunted. "You got away lucky." He walked to where Carlita waited. She'd been untied and her black eyes searched his face, saw the coldness in it.

"It's a long way back to Condor," she said.

"You'll find your way," he said curtly.

Her eyes reached out to him. "I could go on with you, Fargo. It was good with me, wasn't it?"

The big man's eyes stayed blue shale. "Yes, you're good at laying and at lying. Get your horse and ride out of here before I change my mind and tie you up for the Mescaleros to find," he said.

She read his face and knew it was done with; she half-shrugged, turned, and walked to her horse without another word. Fargo watched her mount, ride slowly away, and he went back to the others. Fern stood alone, her face still showing aftershock, and Fargo waited as Vander had his troopers find a place to bury the dead. When they were ready to move on, the sun was high in the sky, and it was a silent and sober group.

"I think I should go after Bracca," Vander said to Fargo with more reluctance than enthusiasm. "He might try to ambush us."

"With only five of his vaqueros left?" Fargo said. "No, he's still high-tailing it. He's a second-rate *bandido*, the kind who knows how to run best."

He led the group forward, moving down from the high rock hills at the first passage. Fern rode alone, behind him, her face grave, but he felt her eyes watching him. She was there when he halted to examine a set of tracks. "Two packhorses, three more riders," Fargo said.

"Vilas, all right," Vander said. "We're on his tail. How old are they?"

Fargo ran his hand across the imprints, lifted them up, and examined the dirt on the bottom of his fingertips. "Dry," he grunted. "At least two or three days." He swung onto the pinto and followed the trail, going down to the base of the hills. The land widened and he espied the Rio Grande snaking its way along the Texas-Mexico border. The hills grew greener alongside the river, stands of willow and black walnut. By dusk he had moved into a series of low, rolling hills. The hoofprints had appeared often enough and he pointed out a spot where the riders had camped and let the horses graze on fescue grasses a few yards away. He found a small hollow and halted, the dark coming on quickly.

"Camp here," he said. "After we eat, I'm going up higher. I want a long look around when dawn breaks."

Vander saw to his troopers as Boswell made a small fire and Fern broke out beans to cook and mix with hardtack. Fargo unsaddled the pinto, had just finished when Herbst and Crane sauntered over. "Think we're gaining on him?" Crane asked.

Fargo nodded. "We could be real near in another day," he said.

"You know, we were very impressed by the way you handled that business with those *bandidos*," Herbst said. "Frankly, if you hadn't come up with a plan, there would have been hell to pay."

"Probably," Fargo agreed, smoothing the cinch down as he put the saddle on the ground.

"Just between us," Herbst began, lowering his voice further. "The lieutenant feels that the way to nail Vilas is to bull his way in. We think that could be disaster. If you could get to that saddle first and see that it gets in our hands, we'd make it worth your while."

"I see," Fargo said, pursing his lips. "It's something to think about."

"Please do think about it, Fargo. We'll see that you're properly taken care of," Herbst said.

"It's not that we're not all cooperating, you understand," Crane added. "It's just that the lieutenant is so eager, the impetuousness of a young officer. We wouldn't want him to send Vilas running after we've come this close."

"I understand," Fargo said, tossed them a pleasant smile. "I'll let you know."

The two men nodded, went off together. Fargo

strolled to the fire, took a tin plate of food from Boswell, and ate quickly. He saw Fern staying to herself, her face still grave, and he finished the meal, took the saddle with him, and started to climb into the thicker stand of black walnut. He gave a soft whistle and the pinto followed as he climbed to a place where a small flat ledge jutted half over the hill and looked down on the night-covered land. He laid out his bedroll and let the pinto graze on the rabbit brush that grew nearby, their thousands of tiny yellow flowers a favorite of elk and mountain sheep. He lay down, stretched his body, and thought about Crane and Herbst, and a small smile edged over his lips. Things were shaping up exactly as he'd thought they would. As it seemed that Vilas and the saddle were coming within reach, the separate moves were starting to take shape. That damn saddle held something more important to each of them than the phony stories they'd fed him. Herbst and Crane had been first. But they wouldn't be last, he wagered with a silent chuckle. A twig snapped and he sat up, his hand on the Colt instantly.

He rolled on his side, drew the revolver, listened again. He heard brush being pushed aside, no attempt at stealth. "Fargo?" the voice called out, and he pushed the gun back into its holster.

"Over here," he said, and watched her come into view through the trees. She walked to where he sat on the bedroll and he saw her face still wore a hint of perplexity. She halted before him, sank down onto her knees at the edge of the bedroll, the slenderness of her body suddenly very apparent. Perhaps because he'd been thinking about Carlita. "Come to talk about the saddle?" he asked casually.

Her brows lifted a fraction. "The saddle? No," she said. "I came to talk about this morning." She paused, her eyes holding on him. "You made it all come off. I know that," she said solemnly. "I'll always remember that."

"I imagine you will," he said.

She studied his face, her eyes moving over the strong, intense handsomeness of it. "You're a man of constant surprises, Fargo," she said.

"Because of this morning?" he asked. "Hell, it was worth a try."

"Not just that. How come you haven't even hinted at my being grateful?" she asked.

"I figure you're that," he said mildly.

"You know what I mean," Fern replied. "You've made enough tries before this, and now, when I'm really in your debt, you don't even give it a try."

"You disappointed?" he slid at her.

The cool aloofness came into her face at once. "Surprised," she said. "I'm surprised, that's all."

He kept the smile inside himself as he answered. "An old friend of mine used to say, 'Who wants mutton after you've been having good, sweet quail?'"

He watched her eyes widen, her lips part, and the fury start to color her face. "You bastard, Fargo. You rotten bastard," she hissed. She moved, straightened, flung herself at him, and he felt her mouth pressing on his. "Mutton, you bastard. I'll show you who's mutton," she raged.

Her mouth pressed hard, and he felt her tongue pushing into his mouth, darting, pressing, circling wildly. He felt her hand tearing at the blouse, pulling it open, and he half-turned, flipped her on her back roughly, and she let out a little gasp. His eyes went down to the open blouse and her breasts thrusting upward, full enough, so very different from the round breasts of Carlita. Fern's very white twin mounds were upturned, tiny nipples pointing saucily, very pink little circles around each. She wriggled, shook the blouse off, her hands pulling at his head, pressing him down to her. She moved and pushed one breast into his lips, and he felt her hands trying to unbutton his trousers, take off his gun belt. He helped her and in moments she was naked against his hard, lean body, and she half-climbed over him, pressing first one, then the other breast into his mouth.

"Goddamn you," he heard her gasp. "Oh, Jesus . . . oh, goddamn you. Oh, oh . . . oooh." Her hands reached down for him and she found him and a yelp came from her, pure delight, and she pulled feverishly on him as her mouth worked on his, her breath coming in tiny, half-choked sounds. "You . . . you . . . oh, God . . . oh, God." She whirled herself half-around, flung herself across his abdomen, and he felt the sweet wetness of her mouth close around him. In between curses, she made soft little noises of ecstasy, finally stopping to catch her breath. He pulled her around as she drew in deep gasps of air, almost flung her on the ground and thrust into her. "Aaaaaiiii . . ." she half-screamed, and then, instantly, she was writhing, lifting, heaving against him, her long legs flailing back and forth against his ribs.

"Bastard . . . aaaaah . . . oh, Jesus . . . more . . . oh, more . . . bastard . . ." The sounds were coming from her in a wild mixture of fury and ecstasy, a rushing tide of emotions that swept him along, and he heard his own cry of delight as she matched his every move, urged him to more, became a fervent, thirsting, hungering creature consumed with only one thing. He felt the already wild thrustings of her suddenly grow frantic. Her surrogate lips seemed to clasp tighter around him and she was making tiny sounds inside her throat, and the franticness gave way to an eruption of the senses. She dug her heels into the ground, lifted, and held him for that endless instant; and her cry was almost a strangled sound, but it ended too soon, as always, and he felt himself flow down with her, satisfied and spent. And he stayed with her, inside her enveloping grip as she pressed her legs around him.

He let his gaze take in the beauty of her: small waist, ribs just showing enough, a flat abdomen, and a small but tightly grown little nap that, he saw for the first time, was a reddish brown. Finally he drew back from her and she opened her eyes as he settled beside her, rose up on one elbow, and he saw the fire in their softness.

"Was that mutton, damn you?" She glared.

He let the smile slide across his face. "No, that was pretty damn good," he admitted, and watched the glare fade from her eyes, tiny lights of smug satisfaction take its place. "Unless it was an accident," he added idly.

"Damn you," she snapped, leaned over him, her mouth opening for him. She swung over his body, lifted herself, pressed the red-blond little triangle against him as she put one saucy breast into his mouth. He came ready almost instantly and she proceeded to prove there had been no accident, no passing happenstance.

Later, he lay beside her and she leaned her breasts over his chest, her eyes on the half-moon scar of his forearm as she traced her fingers across it. "Some woman who refused to let you have your way?" she asked.

"Sort of." He chuckled. "A she-grizzly who had her own ideas about eating me."

Fern's lips moved to rest lightly against one of the nipples on his chest. "I know now why I detested that little Mexican package," she half-whispered. "I must've known, inside, you'd be like this."

"Next time be more honest with yourself," Fargo told her.

"Maybe and maybe not. Honesty can frighten. It's like abdicating your own willpower," she said.

"Then I guess you'll have to decide," Fargo remarked.

"Decide what?" she frowned back.

"Whether it's better to be satisfied or scared," he said.

"I think that's been decided," she said thoughtfully, putting her hands on his chest. "How close are we to Vilas?" she asked slowly.

He held his answer for a moment, decided to put his thought into words. "You thinking about the saddle or screwing?" he asked mildly.

"Dammit, must you always put everything so crudely?" she flared, half sitting up.

He laughed. "Only because you still need facing yourself," he told her. He watched her, waited for an answer.

"Maybe both," she tossed back. She knew how to fence and was probably being honest, he decided.

"Too close," he said. "Want me to slow down?"

"No," she blurted out, and the excitement and dismay he saw struggle in her face were both real. "No, get that saddle. We can make up for it afterward," she said, leaning back over him.

"Whatever you say," Fargo agreed. "Anything more you want to tell me about why you're after that saddle?" he asked.

She sat up and he caught an instant wariness come into her eyes. "No, I told you everything. What makes you ask that?" she questioned.

"No special reason," he answered. "I just thought maybe there was something you'd forgotten to mention."

She looked away, reached out for her blouse, and started to slip into it, and he watched her upturned breasts lift and dip in beautiful motion. "Maybe, after I've the saddle, we can talk more," she said quietly, pulled on her trousers, bent down to him, her arms sliding around his neck. "Come with me when this is finished, Fargo," she said. He kept the smile inside himself. When this was finished she'd be mad as a hornet.

"Why?" he asked.

"There'll be reasons enough, good ones. I'll tell you

then," she said. He grunted inwardly, wagered that they'd tie in with why she was after the saddle.

"I've my own way to go, my own things to finish," he told her.

"Such as?" she pressed.

"I had a family once. Three murdering gunslingers took care of that, my pa, my ma and my kid brother. Only one has paid so far. There are two to go," he said.

"Maybe you'll never find them," she said.

"I'll find them," he said, a terribly finality coming into his voice. "Somewhere, someplace, I'll find them."

"Make a detour, with me, Fargo," she said, a hint of excitement touching her voice and she kissed him. "We'll talk more about it when the time comes," she said.

He studied her eyes. Something had stirred her, excited her. "When the time comes," he echoed, saw her smile with happy confidence.

"I'd better get back," she said, pulling away, finishing with her blouse, pulling it tight against the upturned breasts as she tucked it into her waistband.

"Can't have the neighbors gossiping," Fargo said.

"Find a place for us tomorrow night," she half-whispered, as desire flooded into her voice.

"I'll try," he told her and watched as she blew a kiss at him as she hurried away, a slender shape disappearing into the trees. He leaned back and allowed the smile to slide over his face. She was staying with her story, continuing to lie about the saddle. Not the same kind of lying as Carlita's, he was certain, none of the personal fury in it. Something else. Principle instead of wilfullness. Or money instead of possessiveness. But she was lying, along with all the others. Only on his bedroll had she been honest. But Carlita had been honest there, too, he reminded himself. They were so different in every other respect: Carlita—full-figured, fleshy, all sensual throbbing; Fern—slender curves, soft firmness, all steel-wire pulsating. Yet both twisted truth to their own ends. Carlita had paid. Fern had yet to learn the price.

He closed his eyes and slept until morning and got everyone off to an early start. He was becoming impatient. The tracks of the three riders and the two pack horses grew stronger and he pointed them out to the others. During a midday break, as he sat alone beside the Ovaro, Vander came up and folded himself nearby on the ground.

"I haven't made an issue of it but of course you know that the army has first call on that saddle and the documents in it," the lieutenant said, trying unsuccessfully to sound matter-of-fact.

Fargo let his eyebrows lift. "No, I didn't know that," he said.

"Oh, indeed. Official government business always takes precedence over any civilian demands," the lieutenant said with his usual pompousness. "It's your duty to put that saddle in my hands first, Fargo," he added.

"My duty?" Fargo frowned back.

"Why, yes, as a citizen, it's your duty to support the government and I represent that government in this," Vander said.

"Mister Lieutenant Vander, my only duty is staying alive and getting paid for my work," Fargo said.

Vander licked his lips. "I expected that might be your attitude," he said. "If you put that saddle in my hands, I'm authorized to tell you that the army will double the amount you're being paid now."

"Well, now, that puts a different light on duty." Fargo grinned.

"Yes, I thought you'd see that," Vander said, and was unable to hide the disapproval in his tone.

"I'll give that some thought," Fargo said, and Vander pulled himself to his feet, nodded stiffly, and strode back to his troopers.

Fargo laughed inside himself. Two out of three. That left only one strawberry-blond bombshell. He was almost certain she'd not disappoint him. He rose and led the party off again, riding until dusk came, halted at a flat place against a sheet of high stone at their backs. Fern frowned at him as he unsaddled the pinto.

"There's no damn place to be alone here," she whispered.

He shrugged apologetically. "I know, but that's how it fell," he said, and her frown stayed. "You said we could make up after you got the saddle."

Her eyes met his and she nodded, let the frown slide from her face. "Yes, you can count on that," she said. "I guess this wanting business is hard to put aside, though."

He tossed her a grin, put the saddle on the ground as the darkness came to blanket the camp. She slid down beside him as he laid out his bedroll, leaned against him, her body warm, soft, and made of promise. "One thing, before I go back to my bedroll," she began. "It's about the saddle."

"What about the saddle?" he asked innocently.

"Will you help me, Fargo? I have to have it in my hands first," she said.

He let himself sound surprised. "Why?"

"If the others get hold of it, they'll hang on to it for God knows how long. Herbst and Crane will bring it back for evidence and the bank will have all kinds of legal formalities. The lieutenant will have to return it until all the formal army reports and hearings are over. That'll all take months. I can't wait that long. I just want the saddle in Boswell's hands and my father out of his debt. I'll give the lieutenant his documents and Herbst and Crane their money, but I want the saddle to give to Boswell."

She sounded so thoroughly reasonable, Fargo mused

with an inner smile. "I'll try," he told her. "Just need a little time to figure a way."

He heard her little happy gasp and her lips brushed his cheek. "Then we can be together all the way back," she said, and the anticipation in her voice wore no disguise. He watched her hurry off to put out her bedroll along the other edge of the campsite. Fargo lay back and smiled as he went to sleep.

9

He was up with the dawn, his plans all in place, and he set a fast pace for the first part of the day. Each time he halted to study the trail of the five riders, all but the troopers gathered around him. "Close, now," he told them, and he could feel the excitement sweep through him.

"How close?" Herbst asked.

"Not more'n a day, maybe less," Fargo said.

The trail had led back into the rolling hills that bordered the Rio Grande on the Texas side of the river, the black walnut giving way to Gambel oaks and Spanish clover.

"Think about what I said?" Fern asked as she rode beside him at one point during the day, and he nodded, tossed her a reassuring smile. He halted a little farther on, where the hoofprints of the three riders and their two packhorses had shown they'd paused at a trickling stream. Fargo dismounted, let the horses refresh themselves from the stream, studied the tracks again.

"We'll be in sight by tomorrow," he said, rose, and swung onto the pinto. "Be right back. I want a look ahead while the afternoon light's still good," he said, and rode off alone. He moved into a stand of Gambel oak, dismounted, and crouched down, moving his hand over the ground to find a small piece of stone. He discarded one after another, finally stared at one only slightly larger than a pebble. He picked it up, went to the pinto, and picked up the horse's left foreleg. He pushed the pebble into the frog of the pinto's foot, along the curved edge of the horseshoe. Wedging it in deeply, he estimated it would take an hour or two before it worked its way out enough to start hurting the horse. He remounted and went back to where the others waited. "Let's go," he said. "We keep right on their trail."

He rode for another hour and watched the sun begin to move toward the horizon line. It took almost a half-hour more, but suddenly the pinto began to go lame on its left foreleg. Fargo kept on until he spotted another clear set of hoofprints, then reined up and swung from the horse. He picked up the pinto's foreleg, examined it, looked at the hoof, set the leg down again.

Fern had dismounted, Boswell and Crane doing the same. Herbst and Vander were still on their horses.

Fargo looked ruefully at the others, letting his glance linger on Fern. "He's gone lame," he said. "He's always had a weak left pastern."

Fern frowned at him. "You can ride with me, let the pinto follow along," she said.

Fargo let himself appear even more rueful. "Walking's going to be too much for him, 'less it's real slow and easy, and that's not what we'll be doing," he said. "I guess this is where I get off," he added, shaking his head, bending down to rub the pinto's pastern.

He straightened up, swept the others with his glance. "But you're lucky it happened now. Vilas is less than a day ahead. His tracks are clear now. All you have to do is follow them. You don't really need me anymore," he said.

Fern's eyes held protest and disappointment.

"Actually, you're quite right, Fargo," Vander said.

"No, you go with us, Fargo," Fern pressed.

Fargo let himself look rueful again. "It's no good. First, I won't risk ruining my horse, and second, I'd slow you down too much. You don't need that at this stage," he said.

"No, we don't, now that we're so near," Herbst put in, and Vander agreed, obviously eager to assume full charge now.

"We can take it from here," the lieutenant said. "Fargo's earned the balance of his fee. I say settle with him and get on with it."

Fargo tossed him a grateful glance. "I'd be much obliged," he said.

"I don't see that we've much choice. We certainly don't want to be slowed down," Herbst concurred, and Vander opened his army-issue black-leather saddlebag, handed Fargo the balance of his fee.

Fargo took it with a small smile and a nod, and saw Fern bent over, rubbing her hand along the pinto's pastern. "No swelling yet," she murmured.

"No, and I don't want one developing," Fargo said.

She lifted the horse's foreleg, let it down again, and the horse plainly put less than his normal weight on it. "It happened so suddenly," she muttered, frowning.

"That's the way it does, sometimes," Fargo said. "I'm going to lead him slow five minutes, then rest him five minutes, walk and rest."

He saw Herbst, Crane, and Boswell back their horses to move beside the lieutenant as he took his place at the head of his troopers.

Fern came to stand very close to the big black-haired man, her eyes searching his. "What happens to the things we talked about? What happens to us? You can't just walk away like this," she half-whispered.

"You're all in this together. You'll work out something," he said. "And as for us, I'll wait for you in Condor. Hell, if I can't get the lameness out of that leg, you may be there before me."

She thought for a moment, her eyes still probing, trying to see behind his apologetic ruefulness. "In Condor," she murmured, turned to mount the gray mare.

"You'll all make out fine," he called to her. "Vilas and the saddle are practically in your hands now."

She waved and he waved back as the column started off, Vander in the lead this time.

Fargo's eyes went to the sky. Another two hours till dark, at the most, he estimated. He caught Fern's glance back at him just before the column disappeared around a curve, waved a hand again at her. Slowly, whistling a little tune through his teeth, he began to walk the pinto back the way they'd come. He paused at the end of five minutes, listened to the silence. The wind rustled the Gambel oaks and he heard the sound of a green-tailed towhee, soft in the upper branches of a distant tree. A scraping noise was a scaly swift making its way along the ground. He continued to listen with ears acute and trained, but there were no other sounds. He reached down, lifted the pinto's foreleg, felt around the frog with his fingers until he located the pebble. He flicked it out, tossed it away, and the horse put his leg down, tested the foot, whinnied and tossed his head. Fargo swung up into the saddle, patted the magnificent black neck, and they trotted off, horse and rider one together.

He rode to where a narrow path branched upward, peered at the set of hoofprints on the ground, and spurred the pinto along the sharp incline. The path broadened, leveled out higher up in the rolling hills, and he turned south again, rode until the darkness began to slide over the tops of the trees. He found a little spot, a tree-lined hollow set off by itself, and made camp. The night air turned cool with the dark and he made a tiny fire, just large enough to warm a tin of beef jerky out of his saddlebag. He ate lightly, lay back on his bedroll, and watched the fire as the Gambel oak branches burned slowly. A spotted owl hooted through the darkness and he heard the distinctive short bark of spadefoot toads. The quiet, steady scurrying of pocket mice joined the other sounds, and the Trailsman put his arms behind his head and relaxed. He'd almost gone to sleep when he snapped eyes open at the sound, a sudden flurry of wings, and he heard the peculiar sharp call of the gray shrike.

Fargo sat up, every muscle taut instantly. The steady, quiet scurrying of the pocket mice suddenly erupted into a flurry of hasty scrambling sound. The shrike and the pocket mice had been disturbed. Something approached. The fire was only burning embers now as he slid back farther into the oaks and the big Colt was in his hand. He waited and now he caught the new sound, slow, steady sounds, a horse being carefully moved through the trees. He waited and heard the horse stop. His superb hearing caught the faint creak of saddle leather. The rider was dismounting.

His finger on the trigger of the Colt, he watched the edge of the trees across from the still-burning embers, saw the dark shape come into view, pause, then move forward more quickly, and he caught the red-blond hair in the dim light of the embers. I'll be damned, he breathed, and watched Fern halt at the remains of the fire. She moved the embers with the toe of her boot and a momentary flare of firelight leaped up as a piece of twig flamed. He saw her lips tighten and she spun around, started to put one foot up into the gray mare's stirrup.

"Looking for somebody?" he said quietly, watched her freeze, then slowly take her foot down from the stirrup and turn toward him as he moved out of the trees, holstering the Colt.

"I figured you'd gone on. I was going to try to keep on after you," she said.

"Show's you've a lot to learn yet. You should've looked around more. You'd have seen my bedroll there by the trees," Fargo said amiably. He halted in front of Fern as she glared at him, and he half-laughed. "Carlita was right about you. She said you were smarter than the others," he told her. Fern continued to glare. "Where are the others?" he asked.

"Camped for the night now," she said. "I left earlier."

"Why?" he asked with an air of injury.

"That whole act of yours, it didn't sit right with me," she snapped. "You were too damn apologetic. Then I've never seen a horse go lame that fast."

Fargo chuckled to himself. Female intuition and a sharp mind, a hard combination to beat.

"It kept bothering me, all of it," Fern went on. "So I decided to see for myself. I started before it got dark. When I picked up the pinto's tracks, cantering not walking, I knew I was right."

"I'm glad you're such a good pupil." He smiled.

"Dammit, Fargo, what are you doing? You're up to something!" she flung at him angrily.

The air of injured innocence came into his face again. "Now what would I be up to, Fern, honey?" he asked.

"I don't know, but something," she said, glowering.

"I just had enough of chasing your saddle. I didn't want to get involved any further. You weren't the only one who came to me asking help in getting their hands on it," he told her, enjoyed seeing the surprise come into her eyes. She started to say something, pulled the words back. "I just wanted out," he said.

Fern continued to eye him suspiciously. "I don't believe you, Fargo. You're up to something," she muttered.

His smile was chiding. "You're being cynical again," he said.

"I'm not cynical. I'm hurt," she said, letting a pout take over her face. "I thought we'd grown closer than that," she said. Damn, she was a clever little actress, he muttered inwardly.

"There's all kinds of closeness," he said. "I'd done my job and I'd had enough. I told you I'd wait for you in Condor."

"I don't believe that either, now," she snapped back.

"I guess there's nothing for me to do but wait till you change your mind," he said agreeably. "But you ought to get back to the others. You're just wasting time here."

"Maybe," she slid out, her lips pursing, "and maybe not. Maybe I'll just tag along with you."

He let his smile widen. "Good. We can make up for lost time," he said happily.

"I didn't say that," she protested quickly.

"I did," he answered, snapping an arm around her waist and yanking her to him. His hand tore open the shirt buttons, closed around one upturned breast.

"No," she gasped out, tried twisting away, but his grip was viselike. He rubbed his thumb back and forth across the tiny pink tip, felt it start to grow firm at once.

"No?" he echoed.

"Damn you," she gasped again as her mouth opened, quivered as his tongue darted into it. "No, damn you," she murmured, but her tongue darted forward to meet his and the tiny pink tip was firm under his thumb now.

He swung her up, almost threw her down on the bedroll, sank down with her, and his mouth enveloped one breast, pulling only slightly, gently.

"Oh, oh . . . oh, Jesus," she breathed.

He pushed the blouse back, roughly tore it from her shoulders. She made a halfhearted effort to twist away, stopped instantly as his mouth caressed her breasts again. He knew anger added an extra dimension to his desire.

110

The fiery little package was still playing games with him, but there'd be no games here. He'd see to that.

He pushed her riding britches down and the little red-brown nap seemed to spring up at him as she wriggled free of the garment; in moments he was naked and pressing down over her. She still tried a half-protest, which he stilled by pushing roughly into her. "Uuuuiiiii . . ." she drew in breath, gasped, and began to quiver at once. He moved quickly in her, giving her no time to gather herself and the steelwire tension that was inside her became a vibrant, electric fire. Her legs fell back and forth for a moment, then wrapped around his waist, and she flung her torso against him, matching his every motion. He felt the gathering of her come quickly and saw her mouth open, her eyes grow wide, almost in protest as ecstasy refused delay.

"No, oh, no, not yet," she cried out, and then her scream drowned out the rest, hanging high in the dark as she quivered violently against him. He held inside her, felt her quivering lessen, and let her come down against the bedroll. "Too soon, too soon, damn you," she protested in a whisper.

"Only a beginning," he answered, and saw her eyes focus on him. He drew his hand gently across her moistness and she shuddered.

"No, not so quick," she protested even as her legs came open.

"Why not?" he asked, the question not really a question as he stroked and she cried out in pleasure. She gave a tiny shudder and her long, lovely slenderness lifted of itself, awakening at once to his touch.

"No," she protested again, but her breathy intake of air was a denial and her lips lifted for him.

He stroked, circled, touched the sweet places, and she cried out as her arms wrapped around his neck and she pulled his mouth down across her breasts. He turned,

111

slid into her again, this time gently, slowly, and she moved at once under him, fitting her rhythm to his. He brought her slowly this time, ever so slowly, even when she began to quiver and her abdomen rose up in a pleading of the flesh.

"Now, now," she choked out. "Now, more, oh God, please now." But he slowed, held back and she half-screamed, pushed against him, tried to bend his control to hers, and screamed half in anger when she failed. She was shuddering now and her hands clutching at him, pulling, helplessly flailing, and he felt her pelvis grow taut, the trembling become a violent steel-wire shaking. He stopped holding back and flung himself deeply as her cry spiraled, circled in the night to trail off into a whimpering plea as the moment trailed away.

She fell back but kept her long legs tight around him, and he lay atop her, watched her closed eyelids flutter, slowly come open, the red-blond hair a fiery halo around her head. She made tiny noises, words without form, and her eyes fell closed again. She pushed herself into him as he lay beside her and in moments he heard the deep, steady breathing of a creature thoroughly satisfied, satiated, enveloped into herself.

He closed his eyes and pulled the blanket up, slept beside her. He let three hours of deep sleep go by, then he opened his eyes. She lay beside him, hard asleep, arms folded over her breasts, one knee drawn up, a beautiful creature totally at rest. He moved, keeping the blanket over her, slid from the bedroll. Putting his body against hers, he half-turned her onto the blanket as he pulled the bedroll free and she murmured in her sleep. He nuzzled her neck with his face until her steady breathing came back, and then he moved away, pulled on clothes, took his bedroll, and draped it over the saddle. He lay the saddle across the pinto's back, not tightening the cinch.

112

Silently he lifted her saddle from the gray mare, carried it in one hand as he led the pinto from the little hollow.

She'd take after him in fury when the dawn woke her, of course, but he was certain she knew nothing about riding bareback. The task would slow her pursuit by at least half the time it would normally take, perhaps a good deal more. He was smiling as, a hundred yards away, he tightened the cinch under the pinto, swung onto the horse, lifting Fern's saddle with him. He rode off, not hurrying until he saw the first tint of the dawn light. The trail took shape and he spurred the pinto on, Fern's saddle strapped to the rear jockey with the saddle strings. She was smart, stubborn, and full of lies, he reflected, thinking about Fern Blake. He'd teach her to be as honest out of bed as she was in.

His jaw grew tight as he pushed the pinto faster. Vilas was close, the tracks clear now. Not the ones he'd followed with Vander and the others but those he had taken note of all the time. The pathway led upward, over a mounded hilltop, and Fargo reined up, his nose sniffing the air. Smoke, he grunted to himself, and he moved through the oaks slowly, peering ahead, saw the spot where a wisp of smoke spiraled up from a campfire left to burn itself out.

He rode to the smoldering ashes and studied the remains of the wood, then doused the embers with water from his canteen. Vilas was careless and uncaring, and Fargo disliked him at once for that. But he was only a few hours ahead and Fargo untied Fern's saddle, tossed it into the trees, and sent the pinto forward. Vilas and his two companions were still together, the tracks showed that much, and the trio were not hurrying. It was obvious they didn't think they were being followed. They headed for the top of the rolling hills. From there it was an almost straight, protected course downward to La Cruzada, where the Pecos joined the Rio Grande.

Fargo rode forward, pulled the Colt out, spun the chamber, and returned the gun to the holster. The tree cover thinned, the sun grew blisteringly hot, and he halted, slid from the pinto, and move forward on foot. He'd gone on for almost another hour, ears and eyes tuned to every movement and sound, and it was his ears that signaled him first. The soft splashing sound of water, then a man's laugh, a short, harsh laugh. Fargo went into his loping crouch, paused to tether the pinto to a low branch and continued on. The oaks were furnishing less and less cover and he dropped to one knee as he came into sight of the men. Behind them, a mountain spring bubbled up to form a brilliantly blue crater.

Fargo watched and found Vilas at once, the man easy to recognize, his description fitting. He was indeed handsome, Fargo nodded, the kind of rakish good looks that would attract many women. Tall, a long, olive-skinned face, wavy black hair, a straight nose, but it was his mouth that demanded attention. Finely shaped lips curled up at the edges to complete the rakish, sardonic cast to his face. It was probably his mouth that attracted women most, Fargo guessed and, watching Vilas, decided the man was taken with his own good looks. There was a preening quality in the way he stood and moved his head, as though even here on this desolate hilltop, he was showing his best profile at all times.

The other two almost seemed to have been chosen for contrast and they well might have been, Fargo thought. One was short, a stump of a figure, but with a torso powerful as a tree trunk, massive arms hanging out from a shirtless vest. He seemed to have no neck, his coarse head sitting atop his shoulders as though it had been stuck there. The other one was equally unattractive, a frame so thin it seemed skeletal and pasty white skin that drew tight on the bony shape. Hollow, staring eyes looked out from a face that could have been a mask.

Fargo let his eyes go past the trio to the horses, saw the saddle at once. It was as magnificent as Fern had described, bigger and fuller than he had expected. Under the silver-trimmed cantle, the rear jockey hung very low and, beneath it, the skirt hung still lower. The *rosaderos* were so long they needed only a short length of cinch, he noted. His eyes stayed on the saddle a moment longer, as if he might see what made it so damn important to so many people. But the saddle revealed nothing but its beauty, and he returned his eyes to the three men. The stump-bodied one was cooling his head by ducking it into the cold water, the walking skeleton was filling his canteen from the little pool and Vilas seemed to wait as though he were on display.

But Fargo swore softly to himself. They were spaced too far apart to take with a single flurry of shots. At least one would possibly get away and he didn't want that. He didn't want any gunshots if possible. All he wanted was the saddle. He moved in a crouch, a short, darting few steps, to the last row of trees bordering the mountain spring. He waited, watching, saw the stumpy one finally tire of dousing his head and shake himself as a terrier would do and start toward Vilas. Fargo raised his gun as the skeletal one also began to move closer to Vilas. He lifted his voice, let it cut through the still, hot air.

"Don't move," he called out, and saw the trio stiffen.

Slowly, Vilas turned toward the line of trees and, full face, Fargo saw the man wore an expression of conceit and cruelty mixed together. The stumpy one's hand started to edge toward the gun at his thick waist.

"I wouldn't try it," Fargo called, and the man's hand halted, moved back to where it had been. Fargo stepped from the trees, moved toward the trio. "Don't try anything stupid and nobody gets hurt," Fargo said.

Vilas watched him with black, glittering eyes, he saw.

"You are the one trying something stupid, *señor*," the man said. "We all shoot at once and you are dead."

"Probably," Fargo conceded. "But I'm sure to get at least two of you. It's your move, mister."

Vilas' glittering eyes measured him and his handsome face grew more sardonic as he half-smiled. "You know how to use the weakness of human nature," Vilas said. "I like that. I do it myself often."

"I'm sure," Fargo grunted. "Now just drop your gun belts, one at a time. You first," he said to Vilas.

The man shrugged, unbuckled his gun belt, and let it fall to the ground.

"Step back," Fargo ordered, fastened a hard glance at the stumpy one. The man's heavy-featured face glowered back as he undid his gun belt and moved back beside Vilas. The walking skeleton had his belt unbuckled before Fargo's Colt pointed at his midsection. Fargo motioned them back further, kept the Colt trained on them as he bent down and emptied the chambers of the three guns, flinging the shells into the trees.

"Now all I want is that saddle," Fargo said, and saw Vilas lift his brows in surprise.

"The saddle?" Vilas echoed. "You surprise me, *señor*."

"Why?" Fargo queried.

"It is a most *espléndido* saddle, but you do not seem to me like a common thief," Vilas said.

"Let's say an uncommon one," Fargo answered. "Now take the saddle from that horse and don't do anything foolish."

Vilas nodded to the short-bodied man and Fargo watched the powerful arms unsaddle the horse, swing the fancy saddle to the ground, carry it back to him. The man dropped it a few feet from him and stepped back.

Fargo saw a built-in pouch stitched onto the left skirt

of the saddle, a flap hanging down over it. "What's in the pouch?" he asked.

"Nothing," Vilas answered. "Look for yourself."

Fargo paused, decided to ask the questions just to see Vilas' reaction. He was more than certain what the answers would be. "What was in it?" he demanded.

"Nothing," Vilas said.

"No United States army papers?" Fargo prodded.

Vilas frowned. "Army papers? I think maybe you have the wrong saddle, *señor*."

"No papers," Fargo murmured. "How about money, a lot of it in United States bills."

Vilas continued to stare at him incredulously. "Money? I wish so, *señor*. I got the saddle from a man named Antonez. There was nothing in it and he is dead now. It's a dead man's saddle, you could say."

Vilas was more right than he realized, Fargo agreed, thinking not only of Antonez, but of Santos, Bracca's *vaqueros*, and the two troopers. How many more dead men could lay claim to it, he wondered. But Vilas had told the truth, he was certain, his answers only a confirmation of the phoniness of the stories he'd been handed. He walked to the saddle and lifted it with his left hand. The added length of the jockey and skirt and the thickness of the leather made it heavier than most saddles. He motioned to Vilas with the Colt. "Lay down, your faces in the ground," he said.

"*Señor*, you have emptied our guns, we can do nothing," the man protested. "You do not need to humiliate us more."

"You're all so sensitive," Fargo said. "On your faces ... *now*."

He waited as the three man laid down, pressing their faces against the ground. He walked to their horses, took a rifle from one saddle holster, another handgun, a Remington .44, from the other saddle. Emptying both guns, he tossed them into the brush. He'd leave them one horse, he decided. He really had no quarrel with Vilas and he untethered the other two mounts, sent them racing away with a hard slap on each rump.

"You can take turns," he said to the three figures as he walked back past them.

"*Muchas gracias*," Vilas said sarcastically.

"Don't mention it," Fargo answered as he headed for the trees with the saddle. He returned to where he'd left the pinto, swung the fancy saddle over the pinto's withers, resting it over his own saddle horn. Holding it in place with one hand, he rode forward, the Colt out and his finger on the trigger. He reached the spot beside the bubbling spring. The trio had already left, the horse gone, too. Fargo rode on slowly, his eyes scanning the ground in front of him, flicking right and left. He caught the rustle of brush a dozen yards to one side and glimpsed the horse, Vilas on it, heading away. Fargo grunted, guided the pinto into the oaks that began to grow thicker as he headed downward. He'd gone another half-dozen yards, the Colt still in his hand, when he caught the sudden sound of a tree branch bending. Cursing, he tried to yank the pinto sideways, but he was too late. He started to dive from the saddle, but the figure plummeted onto him from directly above.

It was the tree-stump figure he realized the moment it landed on him, hitting him like a sack of rocks, and he saw the world spinning away in grayness. He shook his head as he struck the ground with the figure clinging on to him, felt the Colt skitter out of his hand. Half-dazed, he tried to shake off the weight atop him, but the man had one massive arm wrapped around his neck; dimly Fargo heard the shouts and the sound of Vilas galloping up. Fargo let himself fall backward unexpectedly and the squat figure atop him also toppled back, his arm loosening in surprise. Fargo seized the split second to tear free, rolled, shaking his head, and his vision returned. He started to leap up and looked into the barrel of his Colt, Vilas holding it, the sardonic smile on the man's face now edged with cruel pleasure.

"Now, *señor*, we will teach you to steal from us," the man said.

Fargo rose slowly, cursing himself bitterly. He'd underestimated Vilas, and underestimating an opponent was invariably a costly error. His eyes moved across the three men. This one would definitely be costly, he muttered inwardly. The short, squat one could obviously climb like a monkey and now his little eyes gleamed out of the heavy-featured face. "I could just shoot you," Vilas said. "But that would be too simple. It will be far more enjoyable to let Bolos pound you to pulp."

"Bolos? That's his name?" Fargo said. "I thought it was Tree-stump."

Vilas motioned with the Colt. "Over there, where it is clear," he said, and Fargo moved backward to a half-circle in the center of the oaks. "He is yours, Bolos," Vilas said from the horse, and Fargo watched the squat figure start toward him. He half-raised his hands, waited, and the man came nearer, within reach. Fargo lifted a powerful left hook. The thick figure half-turned, took the blow alongside the cheek, and catapulted forward as if launched on springs. Fargo's quick right cross bounced off the top of the man's lowered head and Fargo felt himself fly backward as though struck by a pole. The man's short, massive arms wrapped around him, his head buried into his chest, and Fargo hit the ground on his back, tried to twist out of the grip, and took a short, chopping blow to the temple. Bolos lifted his head and started to slam it forward, using his head like a mallet. Fargo managed to get his forearm up and deflect the blow. The man's face was a grimace of fury as he raised his head again to strike with it.

Fargo tried to push his forearm into the man's neck, saw there seemed to be no neck to hit, and brought his forearm up to smash it into the flat nose. The man grunted, his grip loosening for an instant, and Fargo pressed heels into the ground, lifted, and twisted. The short figure fell to the side, tried to roll back, but Fargo was twisting away, leaping to his feet. Bolos came charging again, the neckless head held low, the short tree-stump figure ramming forward bull-like. Fargo tried another sweeping left and the man paused, shook the blow away, and continued ramming forward. This time Fargo sidestepped, brought a vicious side-arm chopping blow around as the neckless head flew past him. The man fell forward to his knees as the side of his face cracked open.

The man got up, charged again, this time the short, heavily muscled arms throwing furious blows as he rammed forward. Fargo stayed out of reach, tried to slam a straight left through, and hit only flailing, pumping forearms. He tried another with the same result, took a roundhouse blow, then one more that made his arms ache. With surprising suddenness, the tree-stump figure dived, arms reaching out to wrap around the bigger man's ankles. Taken by surprise, Fargo tried to twist away and felt one leg caught by the powerful grip as he fell. He heard his voice cry out in pain as Bolos began to twist his ankle, determined to break it off. Fargo raised his other leg and drove his boot into the man's face. The grip on his ankle fell away as Bolos half-toppled to his side. Fighting down the pain of his ankle, Fargo pressed on it, brought a roundhouse right around, using every one of his powerful shoulder muscles. It caught the man alongside the head and he fell heavily on his side, rolled, came up on his knees. One side of his face ran with red from the long crack down the cheekbone, his nose and mouth were obscured in a mass of blood from Fargo's boot. He seemed an apparition, a creature from another world, as he hurtled the tree-stump body forward again.

Fargo ducked away from the forward rush, grabbed the man's head as he plummeted past, and using the leverage of his long arms and height, swung the figure in a sideways arc. The man crashed into a tree trunk with such force a piece of the bark split. The short, squat body collapsed onto itself, hung against the tree for a moment, then fell sideways, to lay motionless, looking like a giant toadstool that had been toppled onto its side.

Fargo spun around to Vilas, saw the surprise in the man's face. "Enjoy that?" Fargo growled, and Vilas' smile was made of cruelty. Behind the handsome face was a sadistic, twisted mind. Vilas motioned to the skeletal figure.

"Take him, Cuchillo," Vilas snapped from the saddle.

Fargo saw the reason for the name at once as a vicious, long knife appeared in the bony hand. The pale-faced figure began to come toward him but springing from right to left as he did, never standing still. Fargo edged backward but the man was coming in fast, closer with each sideways spring. Suddenly one spring ended in a slashing arc of the knife, and throwing himself backward, Fargo felt the blade nick his chest. As though he were on feet of rubber, Cuchillo continued to spring and now he accompanied each one with a sideways slash of the knife. Fargo threw himself backward again and then again, but he knew it would be but a matter of time before the springing-sideways leaps would send the blade slashing into him.

He flung himself backward again, seemed to fall, went down on his back. Instantly the walking skeleton sprang in, but Fargo's leg kicked out, caught the figure in the back of the knee, and Cuchillo sailed sideways. But he was on his feet in a split second, springing and slashing

121

again, looking as though he were a wooden puppet being jerked one way and then the other on invisible strings. But this was a deadly puppet and Fargo barely managed to duck away from a slash that caught the edge of his temple. In a narrow leg holster he carried a double-edged blade, but he'd be cut in two trying to get it out.

Vilas shouted encouragement, a harsh laugh coming from him as he sat on the horse. Fargo almost ran, half-turned his back on the bony assassin, then turned back. But he had come close to Vilas on the horse. He edged backward, still closer, and now Cuchillo's pasty pale face broke into a death's grin and he came in with his sideways springs. Fargo's eyes seemed to fill with terror as the man's spring matched his every attempt to move to one side or the other. He was almost backed against Vilas' horse now.

"*Ahora*," he heard Vilas shout in glee. Cuchillo leaped forward and Fargo flung himself backward under the horse, rolled, came out the other side, long arms stretching upward. His hands closed around Vilas' leg and he yanked with all his strength. The man came out of the saddle, toppling toward him. Fargo sidestepped to avoid being struck by the falling form. Vilas hit the ground on his side, more surprised than hurt, the Colt falling out of his hand. Fargo scooped it up in one motion as Cuchillo raced around the front of the horse, the knife outstretched.

Fargo fired and saw the shot drive the knife back into the man's chest as the bullet exploded his chest bones. The skeletal figure seemed to come apart, bony arms and legs flying out in all directions. Fargo didn't wait to see him land but swung the Colt at Vilas as the man got to his feet.

"Amazing. *Bravo, señor*. No one has ever beaten either of them before," Vilas said. "Please shoot quickly and accurately."

Fargo put the gun into its holster. "No, that'd be too easy for you," he said, and saw the little light of fear come into the man's eyes. "You were all set to enjoy me being beaten to a pulp or sliced to ribbons. You enjoy cruelty. You're a rotten, sadistic bastard and you use that handsomeness as bait and as a mask." Fargo stared at the sardonic, handsome face and wondered how many young women had been captivated by it and then subjected to the sadistic cruelty behind it.

Vilas' eyes were widening in sudden realization as Fargo's blow whistled in an arc to smash into the man's face. "No more, you stinkin' bastard," Fargo said as he saw the man's eyebrow crack open. Vilas dropped to one knee, shook his head. He put a hand to his face, drew it away to stare at the blood from the cracked brow. The roar came from him as from an enraged bull as he came up charging, swinging a right and then a left. Fargo blocked the blows easily, smashed his fist full into the handsome face. He felt the nose crumple as Vilas gasped out in pain, staggered backward. Fargo's hand shot out, caught him before he fell, brought up a tremendous uppercut that smashed into the man's jaw. Vilas collapsed to his hands and knees, shook his head, and uttered guttural sounds. He forced his mouth open and Fargo saw at least four teeth spit out in a stream of blood.

The man mumbled words. "No, no more, my face..."

Fargo drove his last blow down into the man's cheekbone and felt it shatter and Vilas rolled over to lay spread-eagled on the ground, groaning softly. Fargo took a half-dozen leaves and rubbed the blood from his knuckles, looked back at the groaning form. The man's face was already ballooned out of shape, split and cracked, the nose a crumpled, shattered blob, his jaw pushed sideways and broken.

Fargo leaned down over the shapeless face. "You'll

still be a stinking, sadistic, cruel bastard," he said. "But now you'll be an ugly one. That'll save some poor girl's neck."

He straightened up and walked to the pinto, swung onto the horse, and slowly began to move on. His thoughts were already returning to the fancy saddle in front of him as he headed downward through the hills.

10

Midafternoon and Fargo sat in the little hollow where he'd found a stand of chokecherries amid the oaks. The fancy saddle sat on the ground in front of him and he swore softly at it, his face grimly angry. It was a magnificent example of the saddlemaker's art, made for riding in parades or in the show ring. But it was more than that. It had to be a damnsight more. But why? The question continued to dance in front of him, mocking, taunting. Why was it so damned important?

He had spent the last two hours examining every inch of it and had found nothing, no hidden compartments, no secret pouches. He'd even examined it for letters or numerals, perhaps a secret code that might make the army want it so damn bad. But he found nothing and that didn't explain Fern and Boswell or the two bank agents. He shook his head, ran his hand along the saddle again as he'd done a hundred times now. Even the stirrup leather was beautifully double-stitched like all the other parts of it.

"Something, goddamn, something," he muttered aloud as the beautiful saddle defied explaining itself. "I'm missing something." He lifted it, flipped it over onto its top, where it rested on the ground like an overturned turtle. He pressed his hands down across the smooth underside, moving over every inch of it, feeling for a line, a slit that would mean a hidden opening. But there was nothing except the unbroken smoothness of the unembroidered leather. No army documents anywhere, no stolen money, he grunted. There never had been either, he answered himself. So why in hell were they all after the saddle? The question continued to throb and he turned the saddle right side up again to stare angrily at it. The answer was there in front of him, dammit, he told himself angrily, and looked up at the sky. Fern could appear anytime soon. She had gone after him. Her rage alone would assure that, and he returned his eyes to the saddle, his eyes going over the extralong *rosaderos*, the leather embroidered long skirt, all beautifully double-stitched, no ordinary single piece of leather but each doubled and stitched for extra strength and softness.

An enigma wrapped in beauty. Fern said it had been crafted by her father. Maybe that, too, was a damn lie. He had only two facts. A town drunk named Antonez stole it and Vilas wound up with it. Fargo grunted wryly. Facts that didn't tell him a damn thing more than the phony stories he'd been given. He drew a deep sigh of frustration, tore his eyes away from the saddle, and leaned back against a tree trunk to give his frustrated mind a rest. He looked out at the foliage, letting his eyes wander aimlessly. A tent caterpillar was just finishing its fine-woven web in the elbow of a tree branch. The filmy but tight-knit web covering was a two-sided affair. In between the double webbing were the flattened leaves carrying millions of eggs. The wondrous ways in which nature's creatures protect and hide the core of their continued existence, Fargo mused.

He paused in his idle observation, his eyes still on the tent caterpillar as it finished the top layer of webbing. A frown began to press into his forehead. It grew deeper and he felt the rush of excitement spiraling up inside him. The words, whispered aloud, came as if by themselves as he continued to stare at the tent caterpillar. "Double webbing—double stitching," he breathed. "The eggs of life between the one and something between the other."

He sprang forward, half-falling over the saddle, and ran his fingers along the edges of the double-stitched leather pieces. "*Damn!*" he half-shouted, drew his knife from the leg holster, and began to pry at the double stitches on one corner of the extralong skirt. He cut into the stitches, pulled at the corner of the leather, and felt as though he were desecrating something. Maybe he was, he conceded, but cut more quickly into the stitches on both sides of the leather. He finally had a large-enough corner opened to get a firm grip on it, and he pulled hard, saw the stitches tear apart. The two pieces of leather came open.

"Holy shit," Fargo heard himself gasp. A handful of flat, brand-new, shiny hundred-dollar bills fell from between the leather to float lazily to the ground. Fargo gathered them up, pulled harder on the opened stitching, and more money came into view. He worked quickly but more carefully now, cutting only the top layer of stitching, going around the entire skirt. He did the same with the rear jockey and then the long *rosaderos*. Peeling back the top layer of each piece, he stared at the neat rows of hundred-dollar bills. The entire skirt, the rear jockey, and the *rosaderos* were filled with the money. He began to make a quick count, adding up rows and multiplying. It was a good while later that he sat back to stare again at a half-million dollars in new, United States currency. He had part of the answer but not all of it. There were still a lot of questions. How did they all know it was there? Who did it really belong to? How did each of them fit in, Fern and Boswell, the two bank agents, the army?

He rose, took a leather tarpaulin from the back of his saddle, and unfolded it on the ground. With the double-stitching undone, the money wouldn't stay inside the saddle pieces and he transferred it to the tarpaulin in a neat stack, rolled the tarp up, and tied it securely. He put it back at the rear of his own saddle, sat down, and stretched out with his back against the trunk of an oak. The rest of the answers would be along soon, he was confident.

The day was starting to close down when he saw the flash of red-blond hair through the trees, riding toward him. He didn't move, watched her come closer, ride into the little hollow, and fasten him with a glare of fury.

"Took you long enough," he commented nonchalantly.

"Goodamn you, Fargo, what was the idea of running off in the night like that?" she flung at him. She swung down from the gray mare and he saw her wince. He smiled. Bareback riding was hard on the rump and thigh muscles until you got the hang of it. She halted before him, hands on her hips. "I asked you a question. What kind of a man are you, dammit?"

"I'm real flattered you followed all this way just to ask me that." He smiled at her, pulled himself up to his feet.

He saw her hold back a quick reply, bite down on her lips, choose other words. "I want to know. What kind of a man would make love to a girl half the night and then sneak off and run?" she demanded.

"The kind who doesn't like being taken," Fargo said casually.

She frowned. "Just what does that mean?" she snapped.

He met the probing fury in her eyes. She was as good an actress as she was pretty. "You tell me," he answered.

"Dammit, Fargo, stop playing games with me," she

128

half-shouted. "I passed two dead men back a piece. You know anything about them?"

"Vilas' two friends," he said casually, and watched her eyes widen in astonishment, her lips part as she stared at him.

"You found Vilas?" she gasped.

He nodded.

"Where is he?" she pressed quickly.

"Crawling off somewhere, hiding, trying not to look at his face," Fargo said.

Fern's eyes grew smaller and she tossed him a narrowed look. "You have the saddle," she said quietly.

Fargo's smile was pure affability. "That's right," he told her. "It's yours."

Her eyes grew wide again, delight leaping into her face. "You got it for me," she said, started toward him.

"Not exactly," he said. "It's yours for, say, ten percent of a half-million."

She halted and he watched the emotions flash through her face, shocked surprise, chagrin, anger, dismay, caution, wariness. The last one stayed as she studied him. "You know," she murmured. "How did you find out?"

"A tent caterpillar told me," he said.

"Damn you, Fargo, don't you ever give a straight answer?" she flared.

"After you, sweetie," he said.

She continued to peer at him, her lips tight, thoughts clearly tumbling through her mind. "You knew Vilas was up here all along," she said slowly. "You had us all chasing a false trail, didn't you?" She waited and he nodded, smiled apologetically. "But Lieutenant Vander had that report and we followed the trail of three riders and two packhorses," she said.

"The report was no good. I knew that right away," Fargo said.

"How?" she asked.

"Vilas and his friends were heading south to La Crucada. Why would they need packhorses. They weren't prospecting or trapping. They were traveling light. They could shoot game if they wanted and carry everything else they'd need themselves," Fargo said. "They followed the same trail for a spell. I saw their tracks."

"But you kept pointing out the others to us." Fern grimaced.

He shrugged. "Then they switched off," he said.

"While you let us go on chasing the wrong trail. That's when your horse conveniently went lame. Bastard," she added vehemently.

"Bitch," he answered. His hand shot out, yanked her forward by the shirt front. "I've done all the answering I'm going to do. It's your turn, honey. I want the truth. No more phony stories." He shook her once, hard, and the strawberryblond hair bounced up and down. "You can give it to me the hard way or the easy way. Your choice, Fern, honey," he growled. "Start with the money. How'd it get into the saddle?"

He released his grip and she glowered at him, but he saw the resignation in her eyes. "My father put it there and I helped him. He made the saddle especially for it," she said.

"Why?" he barked.

"Because he was asked to do so."

"Who asked him?"

"Maybe you haven't heard but there's real talk of a war between the States," she said.

"I heard some but I didn't pay much mind," he admitted.

"Well, you'd best start paying it some mind. A lot of folks say it's a sure thing. The South is preparing and they need cash to buy arms and ammunition. My daddy's from Alabama and I was raised all over the South. We used to travel a lot. A few months ago he was approached by some gentlemen close to Jefferson Davis. They needed a way to transport a lot of cash through the Texas territory, past northern troops, all the way up to Mr. Davis in Baltimore. They decided that a convoy with guards would bring too much attention and a courier carrying the money in a pouch was just too risky. A wagon train could be ambushed by Indians and a man riding a stage would be as risky as a courier. Northern troops are aware that a lot of money is moving back and forth to buy equipment."

"So they got the idea to put it in a especially made, fancy saddle," Fargo said, his eyes narrowing in admiration. "Clever enough to work," he thought aloud. "It had to be a fancy show saddle to carry off all the extra thickness and the double stitching and nobody'd go looking for a cash shipment inside a fancy saddle." He gave a wry laugh. "Only it all blew up in your face when Antonez stole the saddle."

Her lips grew tight and she glared in annoyance. "Stupid, shiftless drunk. And then he got himself killed and Vilas made off with the saddle," she said.

"So far so good, but you've left out a few things. How did the army in the form of the good Lieutenant Vander and his boy-troopers get into the act?" Fargo asked.

"We had to notify Jefferson Davis of what had happened. A dispatch rider was sent to Baltimore, but he was intercepted. There's a lot of things going on. Anyway, the army found out about the saddle. Lieutenant Vander's troops were closest to Condor, so he was sent after it."

"Boswell, who supposedly bought the saddle from your poor old daddy?" Fargo questioned.

"He was one of the men who originally came to us' with the plan and he stayed on to follow through," Fern said. "He was going to ride the saddle to Baltimore."

"Herbst and Crane?" Fargo asked.

"The money came from the First Southern Bank. When they heard what happened, they sent their agents to get the saddle. They didn't approve of the way the money was being handled and they want it back in their hands now."

Fargo eyed her with a smile of dubious admiration. "So you and Boswell want it for the Confederate cause, the army wants to intercept it and make it theirs, and the bank agents want the whole thing in their hands. That makes it all even more interesting," he said, and Fern watched him warily. "Just out of curiosity, how'd you get together to hire me?" he asked.

"None of us knew this land. Vander'd only been here a month or so. We knew we needed help, so we made a gentleman's agreement to hire you, each holding to our own story," Fern said.

"You mean a liar's agreement," Fargo tossed back at her.

She stared away from his eyes, returned her gaze after a moment. "Help me, Fargo. Help me take the money back to my father's place. The other men with Jefferson Davis are there. They'll make it worth your while," she said.

"I'll make it worth my while." He smiled.

"The Confederacy needs that cash. Don't you have any political loyalties? Don't you care what might be happening soon?" she asked, accusation hanging from each word.

"When the time comes, I'll make my decisions," he said. "I'm not much for politics or causes. They go on about principles and keep forgetting about people."

"Well, I care," she said almost indignantly, then let herself go soft, reached out to him. "Help me, Fargo. We'll have a lot of time together afterward," she said.

"Where's Boswell and the others now?" he asked.

She shrugged. "I'd guess they're still chasing the wrong trail," she said. He smiled inwardly, her reply too glib. "Help me, please?" she implored, lifted her lips to his, clung to him, her kiss sweet, her tongue tracing a lazy pattern across his mouth.

"Let me think on it some more," he said, pulling back. "This politics business is new to me."

"Don't think about it that way. Think about the nights with me," she said.

"Now that's a lot better," he agreed as the dusk turned to darkness. "I'll get a little fire started," he said.

She watched him gather a few twigs, start a small blaze. "What did you do with the money?" she asked casually.

"Buried it," he told her. "But I know just where." He went to the pinto and took down his lariat, strolled over to where Fern had settled herself before the little fire. He smiled almost tenderly at her as he bent over, snapped the lariat around her wrists with one quick motion.

"*Ow!*" she cried out as he slammed her wrists together, whirled the rope around to bring her wrists behind her back. "What are you doing?" she gasped out. "Fargo, you gone crazy?"

He brought the lariat down, crossed it over to tie her ankles together, made a secure knot in the rope. "Just taking a few precautions," he said.

"You untie me this minute, damn you," Fern screamed at him.

He smiled down at her. "I'm riding on and I want you to stay right here until Boswell and the others get here.

They'll probably be here in a few hours at the most," he said.

"They're chasing the other trail, I told you," she protested.

"You've got to stop lying. It's a bad habit, sweetie," he said. "I'd say they were riding hard this way. When you didn't return, Boswell knew you had come onto something. He had to know it. The others went with him, then, of course, doubling back to pick up your trail, and mine." He walked to the pinto and swung up on the horse. "When they get here, you be sure to tell them that I have the money, every last hundred dollars of it," he said. "You'll be safe until they get here."

He started to wheel the pinto around, the tarpaulin heavy across the rear of the saddle. "Fargo!" he heard her call. He waved a hand at her. "I hate you, Fargo," she screamed. "I hate you. I'm sorry I ever let you make love to me."

He paused, looked back at her beside the little fire. "No you're not. You're just sorry I'm not doing it now," he said, and disappeared into the darkness and the trees. Her furious screams and curses faded away as he rode on.

He rode till past midnight, halted to rest for a few hours and then rode on as the dawn came to sweep the night away. He had stayed in the high hills and he quickened his pace as he heard the sound of water racing and tumbling. Rounding a curve in the narrow trail, he reined up before a waterfall that cascaded down a sheer rock face to churn spray in a roaring white-water rapids that made its furious way down the hills.

He dismounted, his eyes taking in the cascading waterfall. From one side, midway up the edge of the rock face, a half-dozen gnarled trees grew almost sideways from the crevices in the rock. His eyes studied their outstretched branches, hanging over the roaring white-water rapids like the long, bony arms of old crones. He nodded, smiled. It was as good as place as any, and he turned to the pinto, began to untie the rolled tarpaulin from the back of the saddle.

11

Fargo sat on top of a smooth rock near the roaring, churning water, facing the waterfall, in clear view. He had his jacket draped over his right shoulder as he leaned on one elbow, legs stretched out. He might have been a man casually enjoying the sun and the waterfall. He stayed motionless as he finally heard the sound of the horses, but his eyes fastened on the end of the path where it opened onto the waterfall and the rapids. Vander emerged first, his troopers halting half in the trees. Herbst and Crane rode into the open, then Fern came with Boswell behind her. Vander looked up at the Trailsman with a frown of astonishment.

"What the hell are you doing there, Fargo?" he asked, finding his voice.

"Waiting for you," Fargo said mildly.

"He wants to make a deal. He's realized we'd catch up to him soon," Crane said.

Fargo saw Fern turn to look at Crane. "You know, you're both stupid and wrong, Mr. Crane," she said icily.

"Give the little lady a cigar," Fargo said.

"Where's the money, Fargo?" the lieutenant called.

"Close enough," Fargo said calmly.

"Hand it over," Vander said. "I don't know what kind of game you think you're playing, but you're not getting away with it. If you want to stay alive, you hand over that money."

"Not so fast, Lieutenant," Fargo said casually. "First we have to have an auction."

"A what?" Herbst blurted.

"An auction, you know, one of those affairs where everyone bids for an old table or a lamp or whatever. Only this time you'll be bidding for a half-million dollars," Fargo said.

"You gone crazy?" Herbst sputtered.

"Crazy rich, maybe, but not crazy," Fargo said. "You each want that money for your own reasons. You can bid for it. The one who makes the best bid gets it. Ten percent is the starting bid."

"He has gone crazy," Herbst said.

"No, he's one nervy son of a bitch," Boswell answered. The man peered at Fargo. "But you've overplayed your hand this time," he said. "You're outnumbered and outgunned. You can't pull this off."

"A matter of opinion." Fargo smiled. "You've got an hour to think about it. You bid for it or you'll never see it again, none of you."

"We could just blast you away this moment," Crane called out angrily.

"And I've a Colt forty-five aimed right at your gut, mister," Fargo said, his voice suddenly steel. He let the jacket fall open and saw Crane's face drain white. "You want to start blasting?" Fargo rasped, saw the man swallow. "Now you go back and talk it over," Fargo said, his tone casual again.

Crane turned, started to walk back into the line of oaks, and the others followed. Fargo saw Fern glance back at him, her eyes full of racing emotions, the unsorted kind. He smiled pleasantly at her. She looked away and disappeared into the trees.

Fargo leaped up instantly and began to step across the

rocks at the bottom of the waterfall, the heavy spray cooling while it made progress excruciatingly dangerous, coating each rock with a thin film of water. Fargo leaped from rock to rock, moving with the quickness of a mountain ram, took the last two submerged rocks in two half-steps, and landed on the bank on the other side of the rapids. He moved down in his loping stride to a place he had already picked out, a tall crevice between two rocks along the shoreline of the rushing water. It was a place that let him see the entire opposite side, and he settled down to sweep the other side with his eyes. He let his glance move back and forth unhurriedly, watching, taking note of each dip and line of the trees, the position of each rock near the bank.

Only a half-hour had passed when the low branches of trees across the way moved, ever so faintly, but they moved. Another set of branches moved again farther to the left, and he followed the progress of the unseen figure moving through the trees nearest the bank. His eyes went to the other end of the bank, where other tree branches dipped. Somebody had decided to try a move on their own and he amused himself wondering who it might be. He watched the trees on the left as they suddenly stopped rustling. He drew the Colt and watched two rocks directly in front of the trees. Cautiously the figure moved up over the top of one rock and Fargo allowed himself a tight smile. Herbst. He had guessed as much. Fargo's eyes flicked to the other end, where he saw Crane edging up over another rock.

The man peered over the rocks, trying to spot him. Fargo took aim on Herbst, waited, let the man move a little more into sight. The single shot resounded against the rocks and he saw Herbst spin, clutch himself and disappear behind the rock. "Oh, Jesus, my shoulder," he heard the man cry out. "Somebody help me."

There was a flurry of movement, the trees shaking,

and he heard the sounds of the troopers' boots hurrying through the treeline. Moments after, they started back carrying their burden and Fargo glimpsed the uniforms as they moved openly. He stood up, cupped his hands, and called out, "It could've been more than his shoulder," he said.

He settled back and shook his head. They'd have another try. Vander would have to have a chance. It was built into the man. Fargo waited as the half-hour passed quickly, straightened up as he heard his name called. He looked across the churning rapids. Vander had come out with his troops lining the bank, rifles at ready, each man on one knee. Boswell and Fern appeared, moved to the side, and he saw Crane come into sight with Herbst, the latter wearing a bandage around his shoulder, his shirt off. He moved gingerly.

"No auction, Fargo, no deal of any kind," Vander called out. "My troopers will lay down a steady barrage. They'll fire in succession without a break. You'll have no chance to counter that kind of fire all by yourself and you'll be able to pick off damn few before they take you."

Fargo made no reply and saw Boswell step forward. "You can't win, Fargo. Give us the money and we'll let you walk away," the man said.

Fargo scanned the line of troopers. A steady barrage laid down without a break would be too much to meet with a six-gun, even for a marksman of his caliber. But he'd expected Vander would make that kind of move. The man had the army tactical rule book imprinted inside him. Besides, he'd not been around enough to learn much of anything else. Fargo drew a deep sigh and stepped from the crevice. He felt their eyes glued on him as he began to leap across the dangerously wet rocks, under the spray of the falls, and back to the round stone on the other side. He pulled himself up onto it and faced them again, let his glance linger on Fern for a moment. Her eyes were wide, apprehension and uncertainty mixed in them.

Boswell spoke up first. "Now you're making sense, Fargo. the cards are all on our side," the man said, a hint of condescension in his voice.

"Not all the cards, friend," Fargo said calmly. "You want to know where the money is?" he asked, and saw the eagerness leap into Boswell's face, the others echoing his expression. Fargo pointed almost straight up and watched the others turn to follow his finger. He heard the shocked gasp go up, a collective hiss of air. The tarpaulin dangled from the very end of one of the long, outstretched branches high up in front of the waterfall. It swayed gently, poised over the roaring, rushing rapids at the bottom of the waterfall.

"It took a long time and a lot of work to get it up there," Fargo said with mild pride.

"The money's inside that tarpaulin?" Crane breathed.

"All tied nice and neat," Fargo said. He waited, saw Vander, Boswell, and Fern turn their eyes back to him. Crane and Herbst still stared up at the swaying tarpaulin high up in front of the waterfall. Slowly they brought their gaze back to him. "Now, I can shoot that rope in two with one shot," Fargo said patiently. "If I do it, the tarp goes right down into the rapids and it's good-bye, half-million. Nobody gets any of it. You'll all lose." He paused, scanned the shocked realization in each face, paused at Boswell. "That's called an ace in the hole, mister," he said blandly.

He saw Fern half-laugh, a wry sound. "I guess it sure is," she said. She met his eyes. "Damn you, Fargo," she muttered.

"Now I think we ought to start that auction," Fargo said briskly. "At least one of you will get the money." He watched as the others exchanged glances of bitter resignation. Vander, frowning, stared up at the tarpaulin. Boswell turned to Fargo, his face tight.

"We're prepared to offer you ten percent," he said.

"Eleven," Crane called out instantly.

"Twelve," Boswell said.

"No, dammit," Vander's voice erupted. "We don't have to offer him anything."

Fargo looked at the man, saw the excitement that flooded the lieutenant's face.

"You've outsmarted yourself, Fargo," Vander shouted at him, spun around to the troopers. "Get your bayonets on those rifles," he ordered, and the soldiers drew bayonets from alongside the rifles and fastened them into place. "Six of you get a half-dozen yards downstream," Vander ordered. "Get into the water as far as you can."

Fargo watched the troopers obey, push out into the churning rapids a foot or so from the bank, brought his eyes back to Vander.

"Troopers Davis and Hardy, you're going to shoot that rope in two," the lieutenant said, excitement coloring his every word as he looked at the others. "The tarpaulin will go into the rapids, all right, but the troopers will spear it as it reaches them, and pull it in," he finished triumphantly.

Fargo watched as Boswell's lips pursed in admiration. "Brilliant, Lieutenant," he said. "Congratulations."

"I wouldn't do that, Lieutenant," Fargo said quietly.

"Forget it, Fargo. I've called your game," Vander snapped. "Troopers, *fire*," he barked.

The rifles resounded off the rocks. It took four shots, Fargo noted casually, but the rope finally snapped in two. The neatly wrapped tarpaulin fell—slowly, it seemed, at first—then gathered speed, plunged into the racing white water with a splash. Fargo watched it bob for a moment, then sink out of sight.

"Look sharp down there," Vander called as he leaned

forward to search the rushing waters with his eyes. The others peered along with him. "It'll surface again in a second," he called out.

"Hell, it will," Fargo said calmly.

Vander threw a glance at him. "The money doesn't weigh that much and the tarpaulin will float," he said.

"Not with rocks in it," Fargo remarked. He saw Vander blink, the others straightened up, mouths dropping open as they stared up at him.

"What?" Vander choked.

"I said not with rocks in it," Fargo repeated. "I added rocks, more than enough. That's a deep-water rapids. I'd say it's just about hitting bottom now, about twenty-five feet or so, I'd guess."

He slid down from the round rock and walked over to the others as they stared in shock at him.

"You bastard," Herbst said in a strangled voice.

Fargo shrugged. "You didn't give me a chance to tell you," he said. "The lieutenant was in such a hurry to do his thing."

"Damn you, Fargo," Fern bit out, and he saw her fighting back the tears that welled up in her eyes.

"I don't bluff. You should've known that, honey," he said.

She turned her back on him. "Damn you," he heard her mutter again as she walked away.

Vander's voice broke in. "Troopers, seize that man," he said, and Fargo half-turned, frowning, his hand moving toward the Colt. But he felt the sharp point of the bayonet jab into his back, another in his side. "Take his gun," Vander said. and a hand yanked the Colt from its holster.

"Just what the hell do you think you're doing?" Fargo said to Vander.

"You're under arrest, Fargo," the lieutenant said.

"What the hell for?" Fargo snapped back, saw

Boswell, Crane, and Herbst looking on. Fern had halted, turned to look back.

Vander hesitated for a moment. "Interfering with official government business," he said.

Fargo looked pained. "Lieutenant, sir, respectfully, that's a crock of shit and you know it. You were trying to steal a half-million bucks that didn't belong to the government and you fucked it up."

"It was still government business," Vander said stiffly.

"Does it matter anymore?" Fargo heard Fern say. "The money's gone. It's over and done with. It all just went wrong."

"It matters to me," Vander said hotly. "I've got to make a report and I want something to show for it and he's going to be it."

"What the lieutenant means is that he needs a scapegoat," Fargo said.

"It's no matter to us now," Boswell said. "Do whatever you want." He turned away, Crane and Herbst with him.

"Tie his hands behind his back," Vander ordered, and Fargo felt the troopers start to follow orders at once. "Where's your horse, Fargo?" the lieutenant asked.

"Up there," Fargo said, nodded his head to a stand of oaks a dozen yards off.

"Get his horse," Vander ordered one of the other troopers, and in a few minutes Fargo was sitting on the pinto, hands bound behind his back, riding beside Vander and the others as they started the trip back to Condor.

"You know, you're a sore loser, Lieutenant," Fargo remarked idly.

"Shut up," Vander snapped angrily, and Fargo let his eyes find Fern. She rode sitting very straight, looking directly ahead, her face set. Fargo turned in the saddle to glance behind him. The eight troopers were riding in pairs just a few feet back. He tested the wrist ropes. They'd done a good job of securing him. The army was good at teaching how to tie a prisoner. He turned back, his eyes veiled. It would be a long trip. A lot could happen.

Vander made camp when night fell, a place halfway down the hills. He set Fargo off by himself, fastened his ankles together and tied the end of the rope around a tree. Fargo watched the others bed down, decided to get some sleep himself. The lieutenant had made no mistakes this first night. He closed his eyes, made himself as comfortable as he could, and slept.

It was almost morning when he woke, aware of someone near him. He felt the ropes around his ankles give way and he turned. The shock of red-blond hair almost touched his face. "Be quiet," she whispered, and he saw the knife in her hand as she reached around, cut the ropes holding his wrists.

"I'll be damned," he murmured, rubbed circulation back into his wrists as he stared at her. "And I thought you were sort of put out with me," he said.

"I hate you," she whispered. "Jefferson Davis needed that money. But fair's fair. Vander did do it in, and you're right, he's a sore loser."

Fargo cupped her chin in his hand. "That all?" he asked.

"You were going to meet me in Condor," she said. "I'll be there."

"Me, too," he said, kissed her quickly, and she reached out, his Colt in her hand. "You think of everything," he said, and then he was gone, moving on cat's feet through the brush. He circled around to the horse, retrieved the pinto, and walked the horse until he was far enough away to mount. The new day was just edging along the tops of the hills as he halted. He could just see the campsite waking. Vander would be enraged, but he'd figure that his prisoner had concealed a knife somewhere and managed to use it. He'd never suspect little Fern. He didn't know any more about women than he did soldiering. A twitching pussy is more powerful than all the principles in the world. Fargo moved the pinto slowly on, staying high in the hills, almost paralleling the path of those below.

He'd circled away some by noon, was about to take a path that would carry him farther from those below when his eye caught the movement along a ridge below. He reined up, watched, and saw the riders moving along in single file. "Mescaleros," he muttered aloud. They were easy to pick out, long, stringy black hair, almost always wearing a cloth brow band. He disliked Mescaleros. Apaches were no less vicious, but they were clean and lean, the look of eagles about them. The Mescaleros always seemed a scroungy lot to him and these six were no exception. One wore a torn shirt, another a frayed set of leggings.

He watched them move downward, and he frowned, followed carefully, staying behind rocks and shrubs. The Mescaleros moved silently along above and behind Vander and the others, plainly following. When Vander rested a little past midday, the Mescaleros came to a halt, remaining in perfect single file. Fargo's lips pushed out as he followed the followers and the day drew to an end. The Indians began to move downward again in the dusk, swinging in behind Vander's troopers. They came to a halt as Vander camped and night fell, six silent shadows.

Fargo's frown stayed as he moved with equal silence past the Mescaleros, edged closer to the camp. They weren't going to attack eight troopers, a lieutenant, and three other guns, not with only the six of them, he pondered. Maybe they were waiting for reinforcements. He slid from the pinto, edged closer to the camp, and found a clump of brush that afforded good cover. He'd watch and see what the six Mescaleros had in mind. If they got company, he'd see that, too. He settled down and the night grew deep. The camp became a silent, sleeping place, the troopers along one side in neat rows of bedrolls.

The moon was starting to slide down the late-night sky when he caught the movement to his left, peered into the darkness. A figure crawled toward the sleeping camp. As he focused on it, another came into sight, crawling just behind the first, then a third. Fargo waited to see the others, but there were no more. Only three, he grunted. The horses, they were out to steal horses, he muttered to himself, and continued to watch. The Indians were at the camp's edge now and he saw them get to their feet, staying in a deep crouch. The Mescaleros were scroungy, but there was no one better at sneaking up on someone. He watched them move again, crouched over in single file, and suddenly he half-rose from his cover. They weren't heading for the horses. They were going toward a strawberry-blond head poking out from the top of a bedroll.

He saw the first Indian clamp a hand over Fern's mouth, the second one seize her legs, immobilizing her. The third shoved a bandanna into her mouth and another over it. In less than a half-minute she was slung over the shoulder of the first one and they were leaving the scene like shadowed wraiths.

"Goddamn," Fargo whispered to himself as he rose, made his way back to the pinto. He waited, saw the Mescaleros move off on foot, leading their horses behind them. The one carrying Fern over his shoulder had on the torn shirt, he noted. He stayed back, moved after them on foot also, the pinto following. When they reached the top of the ridge, they swung onto their short-legged ponies and rode off, Fern draped on her stomach across the withers of the lead pony. Fargo remounted the pinto and stayed as far back as he dared. The Mescaleros rode down the other side of the ridge, along a low line of ledges and down again until they reached a small half-moon circle surrounded by small-leaved, green-twigged joint-fir trees. He watched as they took the bandanna and gag from Fern, pushed her to the ground, and he heard them chattering excitedly. The one with the torn shirt reached over and tore her shirt open. He gave an appreciative roar at the upturned breasts. Fern aimed a kick at him, which he deftly sidestepped, then smashed the back of his hand across her face. She fell on her side with a gasp of pain.

Fargo moved down to the semicircle, staying behind the joint-firs, and wished their leaves were bigger. The Mescaleros went back to chattering among themselves. The one with the torn shirt won the argument and Fargo saw two of the Indians take up sentry posts, one at the edge of the semicircle, the other beside Fern. The other four lay down to sleep and Fargo settled back, waited until he could hear the sounds of rhythmic breathing.

The Mescalero at the edge of the circle of joint-firs leaned casually against one of the small trees. Fargo watched the one beside Fern as the man reached down, ran his hand lightly over the girl's breasts, then touched the red-blond hair admiringly. He smiled as the man lifted the red-blond hair in his fingers, caressed it. Fern had her eyes shut tight, her fists clenched at her sides, Fargo saw.

The Mescalero at the edge of the trees was still looking over at the one beside Fern, still smiling, as Fargo's arm closed around his throat, pressed hard. The Indian's mouth opened but no sound came from it as Fargo crushed in his windpipe. Fargo let him sink slowly to the ground. The Indian with Fern had his back to him and Fargo crossed the small space in two long, crouching strides. His Colt came down on the man's head and the Indian collapsed, but Fargo cursed under his breath as he heard the cracking sound of the blow. He'd hoped the Indian's thick, stringy black hair would cushion the sound, but it hadn't and he wasn't the only one to hear it.

He whirled as the other four came awake. He fired twice and two never reached their feet, their bodies jerking upward and then falling back. He spun, fired at the third form hurtling at him, but the shot just grazed the man's head. The hurtling shape slammed into him and he went backward, saw the Indian start to bring a knife down in a sideways sweep of one arm.

Fargo twisted away and the knife plunged into the ground a fraction of an inch from his ear. The man pulled the blade back, started to try again when Fargo's gun fired twice, the barrel against the man's chest. The Mescalero's head snapped backward and a rasping gargle came from his mouth. He started to fall to the side, but Fargo yanked him back over him as he saw the one with the torn shirt bringing a rifle up to his shoulder. He fired and the Indian's body shuddered twice as it lay atop Fargo. The Mescalero stepped sideways for a better angle and the Colt barked twice from beneath the dead Indian's body. The rifle flew out of the torn shirt's grip and a rush of red from his rib cage started to douse the shirt.

Fargo flung the dead Indian's body away, started to get to his feet when he saw the torn shirt move, the knife blade sail through the air. He threw himself flat and felt it graze his head. He looked up and the Mescalero was diving at him, a stone-headed tomahawk in his hand this time. Fargo rolled as the tomahawk slammed past him, grazing his shoulder. The Mescalero, fighting out of wild rage, spun into him, brought the tomahawk around in another wild swing, and Fargo just managed to roll away again. He let the Colt drop from his hand. It was empty anyway; Fargo brought both hands up to grab the Indian's throat as the man started to raise the short-handled ax again. He squeezed and the Indian gagged, dropped the tomahawk to claw at the hands choking him. The man reared back, tore from Fargo's grip, dived for the tomahawk, and Fargo kicked out, sent the weapon skittering across the ground.

The Mescalero dived after it again, quick as a swooping hawk. His side was stained with blood, but the shot had only grazed his ribs. Fargo hurled himself after the man as the Mescalero came up with the tomahawk in hand. Fargo kicked out as the Indian came up on one knee, sent the man falling sideways. He was on him at once, bringing up a long, looping blow with all the strength of his powerful shoulder muscles behind it. The Indian tried to twist away, but the blow caught him flush on the jaw. He flew straight back and his head slammed into one of the joint-firs. Fargo heard the snapping sound as his neck broke. His body slumped down, his head still against the tree. Suddenly he looked as though he were just asleep against the tree, the tomahawk still in his hand.

Fargo drew a deep breath, pulled himself to his feet, and turned. Fern was a huddled figure, arms wrapped around herself. She exploded into action, flew across the clearing, and buried her face into his chest, and he held her trembling until it stopped. She looked up into his eyes, finally.

"One good turn deserves another," he said.

She nodded, her face grave. "I've got to go back and get my things," she said.

"I'll tag along," he agreed, and held his arm around her waist as he walked to the pinto. Dawn came as she rode sitting in front of him, and he unhurriedly made his way back to where Vander had camped. He heard the tense sound of voices before he came in sight of the camp.

"They've realized you weren't out washing behind a tree," he said. He halted as they came in sight of the camp. She slid from the pinto and walked on. He followed a few yards more, halted in the trees, and watched. The others gathered around her and he could see her talking in short, terse sentences. He edged forward until he could hear Vander's voice.

"You're actually going off with him?" The lieutenant frowned.

Fern put her things onto the mare, swung up on the horse. "Actually, really, positively," she said. "I should have gone along with him a long time ago instead of you jokers. I'd have the money back now if I had."

"I doubt that, Miss Blake," Vander said. "He's quite unscrupulous. I'm sure he would have found some way to, if you'll excuse the expression, screw you."

Fern smiled at him. "Most probably," she said, tossed Boswell a glance. "Tell Pa I'll get home when I get there," she said, wheeled the gray mare around, and rode toward the big black-haired man waiting in the trees. She swung in beside him as he led the way back along the ridgeline. They rode in silence until he halted at a spot where the fescue grass had taken root. He dismounted, lifted Fern from the mare, and put her down on the long-bladed softness of the grass.

"Did you hear what the lieutenant said about you?" she asked.

"I did," he answered.

"It's time he was right about something, don't you think?" she said as she unbuttoned her blouse.

"Definitely," Fargo murmured as his lips found the upturned breasts.

The sun was warm against his naked back moments

150

later as her lithe loveliness pressed up against him. It was going to be a very nice trip back.

It was that, everything he could have expected, each day in the cool of the morning and the cool of the night, and Fern's steel-wire cravings never faltered. But the last morning finally arrived, Condor only a few hours away. He had found a ledge that looked out over the flatlands, rock hills to the back of it, and the morning breeze blew across. A thin coating of rock dust covered the ledge and he lay on the bedroll with her, making the moment last as long as possible. She clutched at him as she had every night, hands digging into his back as he moved inside her, matching the quivering rhythm of her hips as she pushed against him faster and faster. The scream finally came from her and she clung to him as a wet leaf clings to a stone until finally, eyes closed, she sank back. The totality of the moment was still with him, all senses entirely consumed, everything but pleasure blotted from body and mind. And then he felt the object in the small of his back as he still lay inside her warmth, hard and cold, the muzzle of a gun barrel.

The pressure increased against his back and he felt himself grow taut. Fern opened her eyes and he saw her stare past his shoulder, her eyes grow wide, horror stark in their blue depths. The scream tore from her as he drew out of her, half-turned, and the rifle pressed into his groin now. He looked up into the face that had brought the scream from her, nose flattened almost beyond recognition as a nose, the jaw bulged at one side, a face twisted and misshapen and still scarred with cuts.

"I picked up your trail almost a week ago," the face said through thickened lips. "I been following ever since."

Fern pushed backward on her elbows, her lips still parted in shock as she stared at the man.

Fargo shifted onto his back, resting on one elbow. The

rifle had moved to press against his organs. He saw Fern look at him, her eyes filled with questions. Who? What? her lips almost asked, the words swimming in her eyes.

"Unfinished business," Fargo said softly.

"Yes," the misshapen face said. "And I'm going to finish it. I'm going to do what you did to me. I'm going to blow your *huevos* off, then your hands, then your kneecaps."

Fargo felt the helplessness, compounded by his nakedness. He stared at the man and cursed himself for not having finished him once and for all. He saw the thickened lips pull back, the man's finger start to tighten on the trigger. Out of the corner of his eyes he caught the sudden movement, saw the handful of rock dust sail into the man's face as Fern flung her hand up.

Vilas spun around, clawed at his eyes. Fargo kicked out instantly, hitting the rifle away. The gun went off, the shot into the air harmless, and Fargo brought the man down with a tackle around his knees. He drove a blow into the misshapen face and the man groaned, fell back, tried to bring the rifle around. Fargo seized hold of it, twisted, and the gun came out of the man's hands. The figure charged at him as he swung the gun, fired. The figure staggered back, staggered back again, still standing, a powder-blackened hole forming in its chest. Fargo swung the butt of the rifle. It caught the man's jaw and the figure toppled backward over the edge of the ledge. There was no sound as it plummeted to the hard soil a hundred feet below. Fargo threw the rifle after it and turned to Fern.

She rose to her feet, looking improperly beautiful, only her face reflecting what had just happened. "Vilas?" she breathed, and he nodded. The unfinished business was finished.

"It's time to go on," he said, and she nodded, reached

for her clothes. They reached Condor a few hours later. It hadn't ended quite the way he'd planned, he allowed.

"I'll remember all the other times," she told him. "Come with me, Fargo?" she said. "Stay?"

He shook his head. He had his own causes to finish. He hadn't time for any new ones, not her kind. "Maybe it'll all blow over," he told her. "We might meet somewhere again."

"I'll keep thinking that," she told him. "I should hate you. You've stopped me from doing what I wanted to do. You won't stay with me. You've made it so that something I believe in has been hurt. You've done everything wrong except one thing. Why don't I hate you?" she asked.

"Because maybe that's the only thing that really counts, ever, anytime, anywhere," he said.

She turned the gray mare and rode slowly away. "Maybe it is, damn you," he heard her mutter, and he laughed as he sent the pinto down the other road.

LOOKING FORWARD

**The following is the opening section
from the next novel in the exciting new
Trailsman series from Signet:**

THE TRAILSMAN #10: SLAVE HUNTER

*The Kansas Territory just before Statehood—
a divided land—half free and half slave.*

"Ah, shit," Fargo swore softly as he watched the scene
unfold. He'd come out to relax in the warm afternoon
sun, to sit under the tree and do nothing except enjoy
the roast beef sandwich he'd brought with him. And
clear last night's bourbon out of his head. Just sit and
relax, maybe snooze a little. But the spring wagon with
the wooden dasher had come racing over the hill, four
horseman riding hell-for-leather after it. A girl held the
reins of the wagon, driving furiously, and beside her, an
elderly, gray-haired black man hunched low in the seat.
"Shit," Fargo muttered again as he took another bite of
his sandwich. Whatever it was, he wasn't interested, he
told himself as he sat against the tree, utterly relaxed and
unmoving.

The girl could drive, he noted, holding the racing
wagon under control as it careened down the long,
sloping hillside. He could see her better now, long
brown hair streaming out behind her in the wind. The
elderly, gray-haired black man half-turned to cast a
quick glance at the pursuers who were closing fast. The
wagon was halfway down the slope when the four riders
spread out to box it in. Two raced past it to the horse
and the other two hung back at the tail. One of the men
reached out to seize the horse's cheek-strap and the girl

lashed out with the whip. The man let go of the bridle and veered away, and Fargo heard his curse of pain.

Fargo watched one of the two at the rear. A man wearing a beige shirt and whirling a lariat raced his horse closer to the girl and tossed the rope. The lariat sailed over the girl to come around her, pulling her arms to her sides as the man pulled it tight. He knew how to rope, Fargo noted. He'd spent time as a cowhand. The girl tried to pull herself free, dropped the reins to yank at the rope, but the rider pulled hard and she toppled backward into the rear of the wagon. Fargo caught her cry of fury and pain, mostly fury. The front riders moved in again, took hold of the horse's bridle, and brought the wagon to a halt.

The four riders surrounded the wagon, and the one in the beige shirt reached inside and half-lifted, half-dragged the girl out, then took the lariat from around her. She promptly hit him in the face with her fist and tried to kick him in the groin. Fargo could hear her curses as she attacked, but two of the others grabbed her from behind. The tallest of the four, wearing a red kerchief with black polka-dots around his neck, backhanded the girl twice across the face. "Damn little hellcat," Fargo heard him swear.

The elderly black man in the wagon was sitting stiffly, one of the men holding a six-gun into his ribs. Two of the others seized the girl's ankles, lifted, and her legs came up, her skirt falling upward on her thighs to reveal long legs, tanned and nicely curved. One of the men ran his hand up along the inside of her thighs and Fargo heard his laughter over the girl's curses. She tried to twist her body but she was held in a firm grip. His hand reached the place he wanted. "Hot damn," he cried out.

"Later," the tall one with the dotted red kerchief said sharply. "First things first, dammit." The two men let go of her ankles, the girl's legs dropped, and she steadied herself on her feet. One kept hold of her, twisting her arm behind her back, and the other took the horse's bridle. "That tree over there," Fargo heard the red kerchief order, and they started toward him, leading the wagon on and pushing the girl along.

Fargo let breath blow from his lips in another deep sigh. *Damn*, he grimaced. His would be the only tree on the hillside. All he wanted to do was relax some, he muttered under his breath. In the wagon, the elderly, gray-haired black man's hands were being tied behind his back and a length of lariat was being formed into a noose. Fargo took a bite of his sandwich, was slowly chewing it when they reached the tree. They approached from the side, intent on their business, not seeing him at first, as he stayed silent and unmoving. His eyes flicked to the girl as the man holding her halted. She had a tight-skinned face, a long nose, a wide mouth, and a dimpled chin. Hazel eyes looked out from beneath thin brows, a face that made its own kind of prettiness out of a disparate set of features.

The red kerchief pointed to a tree branch and one of the others stepped forward, tossed the end of the noose over it, frowned in surprise as he saw the tall figure sitting almost directly under it. "Henson, look here," he called. "We got company." All eyes turned to him and Fargo saw the man called Henson step forward.

"Git," the man barked.

The long, outstretched figure didn't move, and Henson stared into lake-blue eyes as the black-haired man slowly took another bite of his sandwich. "I'm eating," Fargo said casually.

"Screw that. Go eat someplace else," Henson snapped. Fargo continued chewing. "You hear me?" the man growled.

Fargo swallowed. "I never talk with my mouth full," he said. "I was here first. Besides, this is the only tree around here."

One of the others cut in, nervousness in his voice. "Boss, we better get on with it. Tracy could be on his way now," he said.

Henson turned to him, his mouth tight. "All right, string him up," he ordered, returned his eyes to the long form under the tree. "You want to watch? You just keep eating and stay there," he ordered.

Fargo saw them yank the elderly black man to his feet in the spring wagon, slip the noose around his neck, start to tighten it. "No, you rotten bastards," he heard the girl scream. She tried to rush to the wagon but the man holding her arm just twisted as she gasped in pain. She turned her eyes on Fargo, pain in their hazel orbs. "You just going to sit there and watch?" she asked, and he saw anger and despair darken her eyes. "What kind of a man are you?" she flung at him. "*Do* something."

Fargo took a last swallow of his sandwich, let a long sigh escape him, eyed the girl. There was a terrible despair wrapped inside the fury of her accusing glare. He let his eyes go to the man called Henson. "Why are you so all-fired bent on hanging that man?" he asked mildly.

"None of your goddamn business," Henson spit back. "You just sit and watch or we'll make it a double hanging."

The man fixing the noose jumped down from the wagon. "All set," he said.

"No," the girl screamed out. "You can't. No."

Henson smirked up at the gray-haired black man who now stood in the wagon, the noose around his neck. "Ain't you gonna beg a little, blackie?" he sneered. Fargo watched the old man's eyes meet Henson's sneer.

In the lined, old face there was no pleading, not even anger, only a deep, immovable dignity. "Finish it," Henson barked angrily.

One of the others raised his hand, brought it down hard on the horse's rump. The horse reared, bolted forward with the wagon, and the shot rang out at precisely the same instant. The rope parted as the bullet tore it in two. The old black man fell to his knees inside the wagon as it sped off. The others turned to stare at the black-haired man under the tree. He hadn't moved, they saw, the sandwich still in his left hand. His right hand was still at his side, but now the big Colt .45 was in it.

"You sonofabitch," Henson frowned in astonishment. "Take him," he ordered. The others started toward the figure against the tree and Fargo raised the Colt a fraction.

"Somebody will get dead quick," he said quietly, but his voice was made of cold steel. The men halted, glanced at Henson. "It could be you," Fargo said to the man, and now the Colt was raised a fraction more. "I asked you a question. Now I'd like an answer," he said. "Why were you trying to hang that man?"

"And I said none of your goddamn business," Henson threw back.

"Because Joseph Todd ran away from them," Fargo heard the girl answer. "From being one of their boss's slaves."

Fargo motioned with the Colt. "Let go of her," he said, and the man holding her arm stepped back, released his grip. Out of the corner of his eyes, the big, black-haired man saw the man at his left dip his knees a fraction, knew what the movement meant. The Colt fired as the man reached for his gun, his hand not more than halfway to the holster. The shot slammed into his abdomen and the figure doubled over, seemed to be pulled backward by invisible strings, then pitched forward, both hands clutching his midsection.

"Aaaagh . . . oh, Jesus, help me," the man cried out. Henson and the other two stared at the big man under the tree. He still hadn't moved, his long legs stretched out in complete relaxation. The hazel-eyed girl's stare held on him, her wide mouth open. The wounded man groaned again, and red rivulets seeped out between the fingers of his hands as they clutched his abdomen.

"He needs Doc Sweeney bad," one of the others said.

"Take him," Fargo said. "I figure there'll be no more stupid moves again, right?" Two of the others bent down and lifted the limp figure, draped it across one of the horses. Henson, one hand on his saddle horn, stared at the man still lounging beneath the tree.

"Who the hell are you, mister?" he asked. "One of her kind?"

"What's her kind?" Fargo asked mildly.

"Free staters. John Brown's dirty rabble," Henson said.

"I never followed John Brown," the girl snapped. "He means anyone who's against slavery," she said to Fargo.

Henson swung onto his horse as the others started off with the wounded man. "Well, are you, mister?" he pressed.

"I never could see one man owning another," Fargo said. "But I'm no part of anything."

"Just a goddamn busybody, eh?" the man growled.

"Just someone trying to finish a sandwich," Fargo said. "Now ride, before I lose my temper, then the Doc will have another customer."

The man wheeled his horse, glared back at Fargo. "Tell you one thing, mister. That blackie's as good as dead and so are you," he said. He slapped the horse, galloped after the others, and Fargo shifted his glance into the distance where the wagon had come to a halt, returned his eyes to the girl. She was studying him, trying to see behind the rugged, handsome face. Fargo let his own glance take her in more fully now, the wide mouth nicely shaped, made for pleasant warmth though she held it grimly. The disparate features somehow came together to form a thoroughly attractive face, he noted again. She held her slender body very straight, narrow hips, and under the shirt her breasts seemed long, filling out at the bottoms with a nice roundness.

"You come on very different, mister," she said thoughtfully. "I didn't think you were going to do anything."

"I kept hoping I wouldn't have to," Fargo said. "Better go get your wagon."

"I'll be back," she said, starting to walk away.

"Don't bother. I just want to relax," Fargo said, and pushed himself back against the tree trunk, slipped the Colt into its holster, and took another bite of the sandwich. *Damn*, he murmured again as he finished chewing the last bite, closed his eyes, and enjoyed the shade of the tree. He didn't open them until he heard the sound of the wagon drawing to a halt.

The elderly black man climbed down, hands untied now, and Fargo pushed himself to his feet as the man stretched his hand out to him. "May I know your name, Sir," he asked, his voice low and soft. "Mine, as you know, is Joseph Todd."

"Fargo, Skye Fargo," the big, black-haired man said, taking the offered handshake.

"I am in your debt, Sir," Joseph Todd said.

"Forget it," Fargo said. He looked at the girl, his eyes questioning.

"I'm Amity Sawyer," she said, peered hard at him again, her eyes moving up and down the tall, powerful frame. "You didn't look so big lying down," she said. A tiny frown came into her eyes. "Did you mean what you said to Hensen, about not being a part of anything?" she asked.

"I did," Fargo answered with definiteness.

"Well, I'm afraid you're part of something, now," she said. "They'll be back looking for you, so I wouldn't keep relaxing under that tree, even though you're some shot with that six-gun."

Fargo appraised her again. "Got any ideas?" he asked. "I'm not much on running."

"Come to my house with us. An explanation is in order and we can talk there," Amity Sawyer said.

"Don't they know where you live?" Fargo questioned.

"Of course they do, but they won't be taking Joseph out of my house, not yet, anyway. You have to appreciate the full picture to understand it. Please come with us?" she asked.

Fargo thought for a moment. He never liked knowing only a part of something, especially when it could affect his own neck. It was like knowing that a cougar attacked but not knowing when and how and why. "All right," he told her, and called the pinto from around the other side of the tree. Amity Sawyer's eyes widened as she saw the horse appear, the gleaming black forequarters with matching hindquarters and the sparkling white in between.

"An Ovaro," she murmured as Fargo swung onto the horse. "Magnificent." Her eyes went to Fargo, narrowed as she peered at him again. "No ordinary horse. No ordinary rider, I'm thinking," she murmured. She started the wagon rolling and Fargo swung the pinto alongside the driver's seat where Joseph Todd had climbed back to sit beside the girl, his hands folded in his lap.

"You can start explaining some along the way," Fargo

said. "Who's this Tracy feller they seemed to want to avoid?"

"Sheriff Tracy. They saw Jimmy ride off and knew what I'd sent him to do," she said.

"Who's Jimmy?" Fargo asked.

"My little cousin. He's thirteen and he lives with me," Amity Sawyer answered.

"Go on," Fargo said. "That's not much explaining so far."

"I am a runaway slave, Mr. Fargo," Joseph Todd said, investing the term with a special, almost prideful tone.

"You're not a slave, Joseph. You never were," the girl cut in angrily.

Fargo watched the elderly black man's rueful smile. "Meaning no disrespect, but Miss Amity doesn't like to face reality," he said. "I have belonged to Mr. Richard Thornbury for the past six months, one of his slaves, as completely as if I'd been one all my life."

"And I arranged to help Joseph escape," Amity said. "It would have worked perfectly, but Henson came back early. We ran into him as we pulled away from the back of the Thornbury place. He called the others and came after us."

"How do you come into this?" Fargo asked her.

The girl guided the wagon over a low hill and Fargo saw the big stand of box elders along the road. "Joseph Todd worked for my father for fifty years," Amity Sawyer said. "Worked, Fargo, not as a slave, as a free man drawing a free man's salary." She drove down the road, swung the wagon around a sharp curve, cast a sidelong glance at the big man riding beside her. "Are you aware of what's going on here in the Kansas territory?" she asked.

"I might've heard some talk, but I don't pay much attention to talk," Fargo said.

"What are you doing here in the territory, Fargo?" the girl asked, and he saw Joseph Todd listening with quiet interest.

"I was following somebody, a lead, and it took me here. Turned out to be the wrong man," Fargo said.

"You're a lawman?" Amity asked.

"No," he said.

"A bounty hunter?"

"No. It was personal," he said.

Amity drove around a curve and the house was directly in front of them, sitting across the road like a giant bullfrog. A stable, weathered, and with too many split planks in it, stood to one side. "Home, sweet home," the girl said with a trace of bitterness in her voice.

"I'll stable the wagon, Miss Amity," Joseph Todd said, and the girl leaped to the ground, landing lightly and gracefully on her feet. Fargo tethered the pinto to a hitching post and followed her into the house, his sweeping glance taking in more details than most would see in an hour. Houses were like people, he'd always felt. The years left imprints. Some showed it more, some less. Some looked forward, others back. This house was a tired house, echoing better days in a hundred little ways, a cracked stairway banister, floorboards that needed resurfacing, a chipped mantel over the fireplace, good solid furniture frayed in too many places.

"Drink," the girl offered, opening a wooden cabinet against one wall. "I can use one."

"Bourbon," he said. Joseph Todd returned to stand unobtrusively in the background for a moment, as she handed Fargo the drink, took a long pull on her own, and slid into one of the stuffed chairs. Fargo sat down across from her and watched her as she leaned back, her long breasts falling gracefully to the sides.

"How about pulling together what you've told me?" Fargo suggested. "It still doesn't fit anyplace."

"There's a terrible battle going on here in the Kansas territory. This is a land divided between those who are slaveholders and those who are not, between those who favor slavery and those who hate it," Amity said. "It's tearing the territory apart. But those who favor slavery are ruthless, have more money, and are better organized."

"Where does the law stand?" Fargo asked.

Amity Sawyer uttered a harsh, bitter sound. "The law? The law's been changed so many times nobody knows what it means anymore. First there was the Missouri Compromise, then the Kansas-Nebraska Act, which made a mockery out of the Missouri Compromise, then the Dred Scott decision, and then the Lecompton Constitution, everything at cross-purposes, everything meaningless."

"Which really means that people do whatever they damn well please, and the local law is whoever carries the most clout," Fargo said.

"Another bull's-eye for the man," Amity said bitterly.

"But that doesn't tell me how Joseph Todd became a slave?" Fargo said.

"My father died a year ago. I told Joseph to go north, that I'd help him get there. There is an organization that helps in that. But he wouldn't go," she said, casting a glance of loving disapproval at Joseph Todd.

"It wouldn't have been right to just leave Miss Amity and Jimmy here alone with all the problems she had facing her after Mr. Sawyer's passing," the man said.

"Joseph went to town without me one day six months ago. Henson and his men seized him on the way back and took him to the Thornbury place, and from then on he was theirs. I went to Sheriff Tracy, but Richard

Thornbury swore up and down that he'd always been theirs."

"It seems this Sheriff Tracy doesn't carry a lot of weight," Fargo thought aloud. "Why in hell did they worry about him showing up at all?"

"It's not as simple as that," Amity said. "Sheriff Tracy's not a bad man, not even weak. He's a confused man who hasn't any firm opinions of his own, so he's tried to enforce a set of rules to keep some kind of order. No lynching is one of them. No raiding anyone's home to take a slave. No trying to free a slave."

"Which would put you on the wrong side there," Fargo said.

"I know that, but I sent Jimmy for the Sheriff to stop a lynching," Amity said.

"He'd have been too late," Joseph Todd interjected. "But for you, I'd be swinging now, Mr. Fargo, and maybe Miss Amity's be shot dead."

"You figure Henson would do that, too?" Fargo asked.

"Dead witnesses can't talk," the man said.

"This Richard Thornbury, he's that rotten an apple?" Fargo commented.

"He's a ruthless man as well as very smart and very smooth. He knows how to look the other way and let Henson do the actual dirty work," Amity said.

"It sounds to me like the Sheriff's rules are broken pretty damn regularly," Fargo said.

"They are, but he tries, and I give him credit for that. It'd be total lawlessness without him here, the way it is in some other parts of the territory," Amity said.

Fargo's ears caught the sound of a horse approaching before the others did, and he glanced out the window, saw the young boy riding up alone.

"It's Jimmy," Joseph Todd said. Fargo's eyes were on the door as the boy rushed in, brown curly hair, a round-cheeked face full of the breathlessness of youth. The boy's brown eyes lighted as he saw Joseph Todd, and his face broke into a happy grin.

"You made it, Joseph," he half-shouted. "You're safe."

"Thanks to this gentleman here, Jimmy," the man said, and the boy's glance went to the big, black-haired man, instant respect coming into his young eyes.

"What happened with Sheriff Tracy, Jimmy?" Amity asked.

"I told him and he went out, took Ned with him," the boy said.

"Ned's his deputy," Amity explained.

"But we didn't come onto anything so he went back and I came here," the boy said.

"Come on, I'll tell you all about it while I fix you something to eat," Joseph Todd said to the boy as they disappeared down a hallway.

Fargo looked at Amity Sawyer. "What happens now?" he asked.

"I must get Joseph to safety up north. You heard Henson's threat," she said.

"How do you figure to do that?" Fargo asked her.

"There are ways. We have an organization in the territory," she said.

"Your own Underground Railroad?" Fargo asked. "I've heard about others."

"It's dangerous, and I'll have to make connections, have everything ready," she said. "Not many make it," she added grimly. "It'll be even harder with Henson waiting and watching. You'll be a lot of help, though."

Fargo's eyebrows lifted. "I'll be what?" he echoed.

"A lot of help," she repeated, the hazel eyes taking on a hint of haughty expectation. "You have to help us," she said.

"Why?" Fargo frowned.

She leveled a slightly smug look at him. "Henson threatened you, too. He said you were as good as dead, too," she returned.

Fargo's smile was slow, patience in it. "Sweetie, if you had a nickel for every sodbuster who'd threatened me and was sorry he did, you'd be a damn rich woman," he said.

"But you can't just walk away, now," Amity Sawyer said, the color rising in her cheeks. "You must stay and help us."

"I did my piece," Fargo said coldly.

"And you think that's enough?" she flung back.

"I told you, I'm not part of anything. I've my own roads to travel. The name's Fargo, not Robin Hood," he told her.

He watched her lips bite down onto each other, and her hazel eyes held more than anger, a hint of despair inside their fury. She ran her tongue over her lips and he watched her searching for words to use as weapons. She was still groping for them when the window shattered with a crash of glass. Fargo whirled, bending at the knees, the Colt in his hand instantly, and his eyes saw the rock hit the floor, roll a few inches. He was at the window in one stride and heard the sound of a horse running away at full gallop. He caught a glimpse of the horse disappearing around the curve in the road, the rider pressed low and flat in the saddle. He muttered an oath as he slid the Colt back into the holster, turned to Amity.

She had picked up the rock and he saw the square little piece of paper attached to it with a rubber band. Amity pulled the little square of paper free, opened it. Her lips parted and Fargo heard the small gasp escape her. Staring down at the piece of paper, the color drained from her face and she stood transfixed.